The Island of Serenity

Part 1

The Island of Pleasure

Vol 2

Japan

By

Gary Edward Gedall

01 08 2015

Published by

From Words to Worlds,

Lausanne, Switzerland

www.fromwordstoworlds.com

Front cover image synthesized by Boris:
encrypto@hotmail.com

I S Print Edition
ISBN: 2-940535-24-8
ISBN 13: 978-2-940535-24-8

By the same Author

Adventures with the Master

REMEMBER

Tasty Bites (Series – published or in preproduction)
Face to Face
Free 2 Luv
Love you to death
Master of all Masters
Pandora's Box
Shame of a family
The Noble Princess
The Ugly Barren Fruit Tree
The Woman of my Dreams

The Island of Serenity, Pt 1 Destruction
(Series – published or in preproduction)

Book1 : **The Island of Survival**
Book 2: **Sun & Rain**
Book 3: **The Island of Pleasure (Vol 1) Italy**
Book 4: **The Island of Pleasure (Vol 2) Japan**
Book 5: **Rise & Fall**
Book 6: **The Island of Esteem**
Book 7: **The Faron Show**
Book 8: **The Island of Love**

Non Fiction -   (published or in preproduction)

The Zen approach to Low Impact Training and Sports

The Zen approach to Modern Living
    Vol 1 Fundamentals, Family & Friends
    Vol 2. Work, Rest & Play
    Vol 3 Life Cycle

Picturing the Mind:
    Vol 1   Basic Principals
    Vol 2   Fields within Fields
    **Vol 3   Pathology, classical, traditional
                and alternative healing methods**

Disclaimer:

The characters and events related in my books are a synthesis of all that I have seen and done, the people that I have met and their stories. Hence, there are events and people that have echoes with real people and real events, however no character is taken purely from any one person and is in no way intended to depict any person, living or dead.

My books are not, in any way a therapy books and are not meant to contradict or invalidate, any other vision of the human being or their psyche, nor any particular therapy.

Notes on the haiku format:

The recognised English haiku format is
5 - 7 - 5 syllables.

However, this does not correctly equate to the
original Japanese form, as they count, not
syllables, but sounds. Not only this, but many of
their words, even short ones, are pronounced
counting many sounds.

Hence, to use the recognised English format
creates a relatively long poem, totally losing the
intensity of the, in reality, much shorter,
Japanese haiku form.

With this in mind, I have chosen to part from the
recognised English format, and settled for
something much shorter, and to my mind, much
truer to the original intention.

Gary Edward Gedall,

Lausanne, Switzerland 03 06 2015

. gary.gedall@bluewin.ch

Contents :

1. Cherry Blossom

Spring arrives
With the fragrant promise
Of Summer.

… "Be careful where you step."

Faron automatically looks down at his feet. His shoes have suddenly changed into thick wedged flip-flops.

His movement also seems to be more restricted, as if he is again wearing the tight stocking over his legs. Even the wooden slats of the narrow hump backed bridge seem slightly different.

Which is, after all, not so very surprising, considering that the small, humped back wooden bridge is only an ornamental addition to a beautifully kept, walled in, Japanese garden.

"Welcome to Japan …"

Faron stops and looks round. Venice is no more; he is descending a small, delicate bridge which is crossing a crystal clear, ornamental lake.

The lightest, delicate fragrances, dance in the gentlest of spring breezes.

The old Buddhist priest, notices the slightly upturning of the nose.

"That would be the cherry blossom, or Sakura, as they call it here."

"You're a man again."

"Yes, and before you think to ask, yes, I'm me."

"Of course I know it's you, but …," Faron stops for a moment to inspect himself. "I'm still Aideen".

"Well, not exactly Aideen, although you do have much of the same form as she."

Faron, takes a moment to take stock of his new incarnation. The body is still the body of a young woman; she is dressed in a tight dressing gown object, closed by a wide ribbon, tied around the back.

She is wearing a sort of 'flip-flop' sandal with a single strap between the second and big toe.

What seems particularly strange is that she is wearing short white socks, the socks have a mitten type arrangement where the big toe and other toes are separated by the way the sock are formed, making it possible to comfortably wear the sandals.

"I'm starting to feel like a weird Dr. Who, or that guy that kept going into the past and would jump into people's bodies. I think that, that the title, was something jump."

"Are you ready?"

"Ready for what?"

"To continue on your quest to learn about pleasure?"

"That would be why we're here, proceed and light the way."

They descend the fragile bridge; Faron has a little difficulty adjusting to platformed the shoes, the tight kimono, poses little problem, his last experiences has made walking in a tight garment second nature.

They approach the rough, wooden house which the garden belongs to. Faron doesn't speak, he is taking in the new surroundings; evening is approaching, the sky is beginning to darken.

There is that gentle breeze, which is now starting to bring a slight chill into the air.

His kimono, is made of light silk, it is
very soft and comfortable, he appreciates
the pale blue and flowered pattern, this is
one of his favourite kimonos.

Already, the personality of this body is
starting to make its presence felt.

He turns to the old, balding monk. "So
I'm here to see if have learned anything
about caring for others?"

"Why not?" He replies cheerfully.

They arrive at the veranda, without
thinking Faron slips off his sandals. Then
gently slides open the wood and paper
door.

They enter the quiet hallway and without
hesitation carry on towards one of rooms
off to the right.

And then, totally unexpectedly, in one
smooth, unconscious movement, he is
down on his knees.

The sliding door is opened just a finger's width, a moment's pause, then, deftly, the other hand twists into action, and the partition whispers open.

He doesn't even have time to see properly what the room looks like, or even who is in it, before he is totally doubled over in a full bow.

It is only then, as he is shuffling into the quiet room, on his knees, that the first shock of the early evening breaks into his protected, inner sanctum.

Dressed in the robes and body of an elderly Japanese woman, is no other than Marie Madeleine!

His first impulse is jump up, run up to her and give her the biggest of hugs.

His breath blocks, his body tenses, and his heart rate races.

He has not realised just how much he has missed her, not until this very moment.

Tears of joy, happiness, sadness and loss, are welling up inside, but yet, this body will have none of it.

She is waiting patiently for the old woman to give her a sign that she might take her place on one of the low, woven rush grass platforms, that were placed over the polished, wooden floor.

"Good evening Rikihei, I am sorry to disturb you."

"Konban wa, my old friend, thank you for coming. Prey, obou-san, please come and sit by me." She then turns her attention towards Faron. "Fukuchō, please fetch a zabuton for our guest."

For the shortest of seconds, a wave of panic floods through Faron's being. 'Oh my God, what is she asking for?'

However, the awful moment passes as quickly as it came. With the tiniest of bows, he turns towards a small cupboard in the corner of the room and hunts out a small, round, flat cushion and brings it over to the guide to sit on.

"Come, Fukuchō, come sit here, there are important things for us to talk about.
There will have to be changes made.
These changes will affect you."
Faron goes to sit, silently, as directed.

"Are you not well, Okā-san?" The old woman did indeed look very weak and tired.

"Ame futte ji katamaru."

The girl that he is fully understands the reference; that, when rained on, the ground hardens. Roughly speaking, that, adversity builds character.

"You wish to speak of something that is troubling you?"

This question holds much in it. It must not be at all usual for this important woman, (as she obviously seems to be), to confide, even in him, no matter how old a friend he might be.

"Yes, I will speak to you of many important matters, but first, what of our manners?

Have Maru bring us all some ocha, the Gyokuro would be a good choice, and you will be drinking with us, Fukuchō-chan."

Again the panic; but again, there is not a moment's hesitation in going to the door, sliding it gracefully open, not forgetting to use first one hand, and then the other.

(It seems, that in this experience, the body of this girl, Fukuchō, has much, much more presence and control, than Aideen had in Venice.)

And not at all forgetting to bow as she
closes the door behind her, however,
inside, a rising panic in her body cannot
be denied.

He watches as she makes their way to the
kitchen.

There is something troubling her, she
doesn't drink tea with the Okā-san, the
Mother, the owner of this house, in short,
her most venerable boss.

Of course he is unprepared to meet Maru,
because, Maru is not just any Japanese
servant, no she isn't really a servant at all,
she is a trainee Geisha. And not just any
trainee Geisha, she is Gianetta.

Of course Gianetta is not her real name
either, but she is the same person that he
met and shared with, as Aideen, in
Venice.

In a Venice that he was walking in, in, how could it be possible? Less than an hour ago.

Fukuchō gives the order, Maru gives a little bow of acquiescence, and Faron returns to the main sitting room.

2. 'There is no wild pig larger than
    the mountain from where he
    emerges.'

**The fruit to pluck
Is never higher
Than our reach**

The kneeling, two handed door opening, bowing, shuffling, closing of the door and waiting to be acknowledged is over.

Faron is finally seated, surprisingly comfortably on his knees, waiting for his adopted mother to finish her small talk with the monk and explain the situation, to her.

However, she seems to be in no hurry to finish her discussion, so there is nothing to do be to wait patiently.

Faron is lost in thoughts and questions; 'what does it mean that I am being brought into this contact with all these people, both the living and the dead?'

'How is this supposed to help me to understand about pleasure?'

And yet, the coolest part of his psyche knows full well that the answers will out, all he needs to do is wait. And soon, very soon, he will find out the purpose of this part of his continuing adventures.

After some minutes, the door is politely opened, Maru bows and brings in the tea.

It is an especially sweet form of tea, known as Jade Dew. She serves the tea to the three of them and then waits to see if she should leave or not.

"You may go now, but you are to wait in the corridor, I will be calling again for you shortly."

Maru gives a flash of a glance in Faron's direction, as if ask, 'what is going on?'

Faron, notices that Fukuchō responds
with, what one could only describe as, a
shrug of the eyebrows.

Maru gives a half nod, as the merest
shadow of a smile, sweeps across her lips,
before bowing to Marie Madeleine, and
correctly, and demurely leaves the room.

She ends the conversation and reaches,
deliberately for her blue, white, antique
china cup.

She carefully takes the cup in her thin,
brown, speckled, right hand.

Without a word, without a sign.

She brings the cup up to her old cracked
lips, and slowly sips her sweet, hot, green
tea.

And then, and only then, places it back
onto the polished, low table to her left.

She then removes her fan from the ribbon around her waist and takes a long moment to fan herself.

"You're onei-san, is leaving." Faron can feel the shock and surprise hit Fukuchō's system, as if she had slipped while walking, and fallen head first into an icy lake.

"Okā-san?" Was all she was able to reply, as if asking the women if she had understood correctly, would somehow change something."

"Fukichiyo, your older sister, has had her contract paid off, and is leaving the okiya."

Faron is again confused, he understands the words, but doesn't understand there implications.

It seems that the term, 'older-sister' is some sort of title and not a blood tie, and that it is not unusual to pay off one's contract, but it has major implications for this house.

"Then you have no Geishas." It was the guide, that gently stated, what was, for all, obvious.

"Yes", she sighed, "without any Geishas to support the okiya, we cannot survive."

"So what will you do?" The monk continued to lead the conversation forward.

Faron begins to understand something of the functioning of this woman, and maybe of the Japanese in general.

She has invited the guide to participate in this meeting, because he has the right to question her, and to ask her to explain the situation, and maybe discuss the solutions.

Fukuchō would not have the status or the right to have that level of discussion with her.

"It is time for Fukuchō to turn her collar."

'Turn my collar? Is that like becoming a 'turn-coat', a traitor?' Faron's mind starts to race, but only for the shortest of instances.

For Fukuchō is experiencing a total state of shock. But not like before, not anguish, nor fear, but a huge mounting wave of excitement.

Yes, there was a spice of fear, of trepidation, but that was nothing when compared to the sheer joy of this news.

"I am to become a full Geisha?"

"Your erikae has already been arranged. Your onei-san will perform the San San Kudo, and you will take over as Geisha of this okiya."

Faron felt like launching himself over to
Marie Madeleine, and giving her the
biggest of hugs, and it wasn't only the
Faron part, that was moved to act as such.

"But I am not yet worthy, mother". Was
all she allowed herself to express.

"That is only for me to decide. Please
invite Maru to return."

Faron politely leaves, only to return
immediately, Maru has been patiently
waiting out in the hall.

"Come, child, you may sit," she is
directed towards a space on one of the
tatami mats, some little distance from the
others.

"Fukichiyo, is leaving and Fukuchō is to
become Geisha," Maru's eyes opened
wide in wonder.

And as has become her habit over the time she has spent in this house, she looks over to Fukuchō, as a form of social referencing, to be sure how to react correctly.

Faron feels like Fukuchō wants to take Maru's hands in hers, and dance, round and round and round.

Maru almost unperceivably lets out her breath, the mounting tension, released and relaxed.

Not knowing what she is expected to do or to say, she takes the easiest and safest course of action, and makes a slow bow of understanding and accepting.

"There will also be changes for you." The head jerks up and the tension remounts.

"You will no longer be the minarai of this house," Faron could plainly see the panic raising in the young woman's eyes.

What had she done to have offended her mistress?
What had she done that she was to be thrown at of the okiya like that?
How will she survive, in the streets, with no profession and no protector?

"You have now been accepted as maiko."

"Maiko? Maiko?" Maru is not as good as Fukuchō at hiding her feelings.

"Maru! A maiko is not a furō-ji, behave yourself with dignity and restraint, street urchins belong in the streets, not in an okiya! Fukuchō, as geisha shall be your onei-san, you will follow her example, diligently."

The okā-san, grabs for her fan, which conceals all but her eyes. Although the remonstration was sever, Faron cannot help but notice that the eyes are twinkling merrily.

He has many fond memories of those
eyes; as a child, he had often been caught
out doing, 'bêtises', and of course, she
had, had to tell him off.

But behind the harsh words, he would
still, from time to time, catch a glimpse of
that twinkle of the eyes.

'We know that you shouldn't have done
that, but I still love you, and 'ce n'est pas
grave'.

Maru, catches herself back, and leans
back onto her heals, but she still cannot
manage to mask the huge joy and
pleasure of this, totally wonderful, yet
unexpected news.

To contain her happiness and excitement,
she can only think to bow as deeply as
possible, so as to hide, as best she can,
the huge and inappropriate smile, the
smile that she finds totally impossible to
mask.

"I believe that you still have duties in the house, which need your attention."

"I am sorry to have troubled you, mother."

"You may leave." And so she does, shuffling out as quickly as she possibly can.

Somewhere Faron gets the image of her rushing out of the house, finding some friends, so as to share this incredible news with them.

Mundane house tasks will surely wait for a few hours, hopefully the Okā-san will not miss her for now.

Faron does not know what to do or say, Maru has left and the room is silent.

Mother has taken back her fan, and is occupied with fanning herself. She doesn't seem particularly rushed to re-enter into conversation.

The guide, is sitting, quietly contemplating, as any good monk would be comfortable to undertake for any number of hours.

Fukuchō breaths in slightly and moves Faron's head, just fractionally. The gesture is quite sufficient to attract the attention of the other two. He then makes a long and deep bow.

"Doumo sumimasen, arigatougozaimasu, thank you, I am so sorry to have troubled you, to have made all these efforts on my behalf." And there he waits, expecting to be excused.

The waiting extends well beyond the expected duration.

Finally, the okā-san, speaks, "Fukuchō, I have more to say to you, and you will need to visit outside of the okiya, later this evening. Please go and eat, and prepare yourself to be seen in public.

You are not yet Geisha, so you still need to behave as a maiko.”

The image of putting on full, white face Geisha makeup comes immediately to mind. It seems that maiko are not allowed out into any public place without the ‘full costume’ of the Geisha.

Faron completes the bow, and moves to shuffle out of the room. The guide gives him a friendly smile.

“I am sorry to have troubled you.”

3. The Cracked Mirror

A reflection is
Never other, than
Ourselves

Faron is already feeling exhausted by all
the events of the evening.

He is happy to watch as Fukuchō goes to
the kitchen; finds a small bowl in a
cupboard, takes some rice that is sitting,
warm in a pot, adds some vegetables
from another and deftly attacks the bowl
with a lacquered pair of chopsticks.

The food is both sweet and spicy, and he
finds it very pleasant on his palate. He
washes the bowl and the utensils, this is
not necessary, as it is part of Maru's
chores, but she is busy elsewhere, being
happy and excited.

He then goes into the washing room, fills
a fresh bucket of water, strips off and
washes all over.

Once clean, he climbs the stairs to
Fukuchō's room and begins the
preparations for leaving the okiya.

Once fully dressed and made-up, he
returns back down the stairs, and goes to
wait in the kitchen. That way, when the
okā-san will summon her, she will be
ready.

Faron is feeling that exhaustion, more and
more, but there is no way out, he will just
have to hang around and cope with what
is to happen.

Somewhere, a fairy bell is tinkling. 'I
believe in fairies, I believe in fairies'.

Somehow it is comforting to repeat this
simple mantra as he makes his way back
to the main room.

As usual; he bends, kneels, opens the
door, sliding it from one hand to other,
bows and shuffles in.

"Good, you may come and sit beside me,
Fukuchō-chan." The added 'chan' is an
always appreciated term of endearment.

"You have been summoned by the
daimyo, Shimazu Yoshihisa." The image
of a very powerful and dangerous man
comes to mind, and Fukuchō begins to
tremble in fear."

"But, what might he want with me,
mother?"

"I know nothing more of this matter,
Father Fróis has been sent to bring you to
him. He should be arriving quite soon."

Maru must have had the good sense to
not stay away for too long, for at that
very same moment, she discretely slides
open the door.

"Father Luís Fróis, begs entrance to see
you, Okā-san."

"Very good, please ask him to come."

The priest comes towards the door and
bows deferentially. He is clothed in a
long, black, frock coat, clearly greyed and
frayed in places.

His carefully trimmed, Van Dyke beard
and short hair, were both starting to grey
around the edges. And, just to complete
the visual harmony, his sad, sallow
cheeks also carried the same greying
motive.

However, even if all these details, wash
over and into Faron's consciousness, they
have absolutely no effect.

For he is, for that moment in the deepest
of shocks; for you see, the person,
standing, stiffly at the threshold, waiting
for the lady of the house, to invite him in,
is no other than Faron, himself.

"Konban wa, Father Fróis."

"Konban wa, Rikihei-dono", she smiles
to herself, she appreciates his respectful
level of politeness. The priest and the
future Geisha exchange slight bows of
greeting.

"Please, come. Would you care to sit,
Father?"

"No thank you, we should be leaving
immediately."

"Would it be indiscrete to inquire as to
why the daimyo wishes to see Fukuchō?"

"It is not for me to divulge the desires of
the lord of the region, my humblest
apologies for not being able to indulge
you."

"It is totally my rudeness for asking, it is
for me to apologise to you."

"It never happened."

"It never happened."

"Fukuchō-san, would you please be kind
enough to accompany me?"

He gallantly offers his hand to her. Faron
is still under a state of shock. Fortunately,
it seems that Fukuchō knows the priest,
but has no strong emotions towards him.

She does not accept his hand, only his
invitation, and so, respectfully leaves the
older woman, alone to the silence of her
own reflections.

The road is lit both by the lights shining
through the windows and the paper walls
of the houses, and by the occasional
burning torch, stuck into the rope holders
attached to some of the poles outside
certain houses.

This gives the whole world a certain, sad,
orangey, tinge.

The ground is only beaten earth, there is
no need to have advanced further with the
surface.

Wheeled carts hardly exist on the island.
This he knows, even without knowing.

They walk on, the silence between them,
neither cold nor friendly. Both know
about silence, both the Japanese culture
and that of the Jesuit church, favour long
moments of silent, inner reflection.

They turn several times, and then came to
face a small, discrete, slightly isolated
house, near the edge of the village.

Faron is confused, this is surely not the
magisterial residence of the most
powerful and important man of the whole
region.

"This is not the house of the Daimyo."

"She wants to see you. I apologise for not
informing you before now, but this
meeting is not for public knowledge."

'Flow with the river, Faron, just flow
with it.'

4. On a Need to Know Basis

Life is full of Mysteries. Why? Is a Mystery.

Faron slips off his sandals and waits for the front door to be opened. They are expected and immediately, a young servant girl, slides open the door.

She leads them into the hall and announces them to the person in the main reception room. The person must have said for them to come in, as she steps aside and bows for them to enter.

Faron moves to the door, he can already feel his heart beating faster, surely this is someone important to them, but for some reason, the image does not present itself.

She bows deeply towards the personage inside, without giving him the opportunity to see who it is.

"Konban wa, Father Fróis, Konban wa, Fukuchō-chan."

He recognises the voice, his head jerks up, like an automated toy. He speaks on reflex.

"Bonsoir Maman, comment allez-vous?"

"Fukuchō, we are not alone. You must remember to never refer to me as your mother when others are present.

Fortunately Father Fróis, has often taken my confession, so he knows, but you must be careful. It would not be cautious if others knew of our secret."

"Oui, Maman. Sorry, yes Aimatsu-san." Faron is once again saved by his other self.

"And just where and when did you learn to speak French?"

"It, it was a sailor that I once met, he taught me a few words, I thought that it might be useful for something."

"That is also why I bothered to learn, but it has never really been of much use."

"Not like English."

"You well know that being about to speak English has been a very mixed blessing for me, Father Fróis."

"Which brings us to reason why we are here."

"Please, why am I here?"

"Father Fróis, has been instructed to fetch you to undertake a specific job.

Fortunately, as my father confessor, and knowing my past, he thought to inform me of the Daimyo's request.

And this has given me the opportunity to talk to you, before you can begin to undertake this task."

"Please, I am not understanding any of this."

"Come sit, will you also sit with us?"

"We cannot take too long, we are attended."

"This will not take very long, the story is not long. However, civility insists that I offer you to sit and drink a bowl of tea with me."

"Then I must graciously accept."

"Takamaru, please fetch the zabutons, and brew as some ocha, and quickly girl, we do not have all night."

Faron was so used to hearing his mother scolding the 'help', it was really just like being home again.

When they were all sitting and the tea was served, Maman turned to Faron.

"You still remember what happened to your aunt?" Faron was nonplussed for a moment, what had happened to his aunt, to his mother's older sister?

"Your aunt, Butterfly?" The father, helps.

"Madame Butterfly committed suicide," he still remembered something of his classical education.

"Yes, Fukuchō, that is why I changed your name, to remind me of her. Only I added 'Fuku', for good luck, you are the fortunate butterfly. She was just a simple, innocent butterfly."

"You have never spoken of this, even in confession."

"I wasn't ready. I might never have been ready, but now, it seems that I have no choice."

"Please continue."

"Drink, the tea is good and hot." They
drink in silence for a while.

"Butterfly, my younger sister, was always
a little jealous of me. It seems that she
felt that she lived always in the cold of
my shadow.

Everything that she wanted or wanted to
be, I would have or be first, and always
better.

It is not my pride that is speaking, more
how she spoke about how it was difficult
for her to live as my little sister."

She stopped for a while to contemplate a
picture of bamboo trees that was hanging
behind Faron.

"Eventually, it seemed that she wanted
everything that I was or that I had, simply
because I had them.

Sometimes she would try a take something that was mine, and if it wasn't that important to me, I would just let her have it.

That was okay until he arrived in Japan. He was so impressive; handsome, intelligent, and he, he fell in love with me. Or so I believed at the time.

We were together for some months before his orders came for him to leave. And so he did, promising that he would return, and soon."

Again, she stops to sip her cooling tea, and contemplate the image.

"He did return, and I was ready to continue my relationship with him, and something very important had happened that I needed to share with him.

But I didn't get the opportunity, at least not then.

She had gone to Shimazu Yoshihisa, he had just become Daimyo, he was my danna, he had bought my contract from Rikihei-san.

She told him of my relation with Pinkerton and convinced Shimazu to instruct me to stop the relationship with him.

She then asked that he arrange for her to be married to him. It was totally stupid, he was a captain, he would never stay, but she was so unreasonably jealous of me.

She knew that I was in love with him, and by marrying him, she would finally be able to steal something of real value to me. More tea?"

"I will serve the tea."

"Thank you, my butterfly.   And so she married him, many of our family were very much against it, but she refused to listen to any argument.

And, of course, anything that I might have had to say, was just my desire to thwart her victory. Their honeymoon was short lived, and he was again … called back to his obligations. 'I'll return soon,' or so he promised.

The time passed, we found out that she had fallen pregnant by him and so his son was born. This information was passed onto him…"

"By my pen, and through my church contacts. It was because of me that he found out that he now had a son and heir. I also hoped that that information would spurn him to return here, and organise to live here with her."

"That was not really what I wanted, but I didn't know what I wanted. Did I want him here, where I could see and meet him, from time to time, or did I prefer that he was on the other side of the world, and far from the side, of my spiteful, greedy sister?"

"Did you continue to see her?"

"No, no I didn't."

"But I did"

"Again, it was through my intervention. I felt it important that the child had other children to play with, but as Butterfly was ostracised by everyone, no-one would allow their children to play with him.

So I implored your mother, in the name of God and all the saints, to allow you to play with him.

It was during those visits, as his mother wished that he spoke English, so as to communicate with his father, that I taught you both to speak the language of Shakespeare."

"So that is how I came to learn to speak English?" Faron smiles to himself, 'I had forgotten that'.

"And so I allowed you to visit Butterfly and her son, on a regular basis, even though I was living with a broken heart.

In all, nearly six years had passed since he had left, before we again saw the billowing sails of his great ship. She was all happy and excited, but what she was not aware of …"

"Nor I, you must believe me."

"He had married a woman of his own land, and come here, not to find his Japanese wife, but to reclaim his own son.

To lose one man that she loved was bad enough, to lose him a second time was worse, but to lose the two men that she loved, that was unsupportable.

Maybe we should have guessed what she would do, maybe I should have forgiven her, and gone to her aid. Maybe I should, but I didn't, and that shame follows me all the days of my life."

"But why are you telling me this? And why is it so important that you tell me tonight?"

"The Daimyo has asked me to bring you to him tonight, because the boy is returned. He is on the great ship that has docked in the harbour this afternoon, and he will disembark this evening."

"But what does he want with me?"

"You are to accompany him to act as his interpreter and intermediary."

"To someone whose mother stole my mother's true love?"

"My daughter, you have been summoned, it time for you to go. It would be disrespectful if you would be late.

We had organised for you to have enough time to come here, and for us to speak, but our time has run out, and you must now go."

"Come, we must hurry."

"Good evening, mother."

"Good evening, my daughter. Don't forget, in public, we are just both linked to the same okiya."

"I remember." And so they all bow, and then the two of them leave into the flickering, orange night.

5. His Master's Voice

The palace of Shimazu Yoshihisa the
Daimyo, is all that Faron could have
imagined. They pass through five Maru,
concentric circular courtyards before
arriving at the keep, where the Daimyo
resides.

Both Faron and Fukuchō are impressed,
so the general feeling is, for once, totally
coherent through and through. The great
hall is massive and, even, being quite
late, pretty full of people.

They are glad to be accompanied by the
priest, who seems quite at ease in this
situation. They walked slowly and surely
towards the far end of the room where he
was sitting, waiting for them.

After all of the surprises that Faron had been subjected to this day, to find himself face to face with his dead father, seems only logical, within the sense of things.

They bow, the priest, from the waist, Fukuchō, fully prostrate on the floor.

"Watashinoie e yōkoso", they are welcomed to the home of the Daimyo, which is the signal for them to redress themselves.   Father Fróis remains standing, while Faron remains seated on the floor.

"Come, sit here, child," Faron has to control the heavy mix of emotions, flowing through his little body.

Even though he has just left one incarnation of J.J. in Venice, his reaction to this one is as strong, as if he was meeting his real father once again. The anger and rage for all the wrongs that he has done to him, bubbling back to the bitter surface.

While she, she is in total awe of this great lord, this individual who holds the power of life and death over every single person in this room, in this room and in the whole of this territory.

"Many years ago, a mighty ship crossed the dangerous waters to reach our shores. It was captained by a brave and noble man. I welcomed this valued visitor, and we exchanged tokens of honour and respect.

That man married one of our woman, a woman of a good Samurai family, a woman of the highest morals. That woman gave birth to a son, a son of our race, of our kind.

That son was taken from us, taken to the world of the captain, where he has grown up, also brave and noble as his father.

Sadly, some time ago, the captain was lost at sea, leaving his son in the care of a local woman, who has done her upmost to install the best morals and values in him.

On becoming of legal age, this young man has chosen to undertake the long voyage to return here to the land of his heritage, the land of his birth.

We will welcome this boy, and show him the respect and welcome that is his right and is our honour.

 Fukuchō-san, you are cousin to this young man, and it seems that you speak his language. Is this so?"

"Hai, Yoshihisa-sama."

"Good, you are to be his guide and interpreter."

"Master, I am so unworthy, surely there must be someone that understands his language better than I, maybe even the Father here."

"The Father has much more important matters to attend to than looking after a visitor. Watashi ga hanasa rete imasu, I have spoken."

And with that, he takes out his fan and makes several, slightly aggressive passes."

"Hai, Yoshihisa-sama, hai."

"Good, he will be coming off his boat soon, please be there to meet him."

Faron bows deeply and crawls backwards out of the main hallway.

"I am sorry but I still have some errands to fulfil tonight, so I must abandon you to your task.

However, I don't think that you will have to face your cousin, all alone. It seems that you have another chaperon."

Faron is particularly relieved to see the guide, patiently waiting for him, just outside the Daimyo's palace.

"Good night, Father, thank you."

"It is always my pleasure, good night. And good evening to you, brother."

"Father." And then melts into the soft golden haze of night.

6. Family Feuds

Blood is
Thicker, when
It bleeds.

"So I'm supposed to baby-sit my cousin?"

"In a way yes."

"What do you mean in a way yes?"

"That you will find out."

They are walking back through the village, the guide is holding a flaming torch in his right hand.

Even with the occasional light from other torches outside some of the houses, and the light that streams through the paper walls, it would still be almost impossible to see, otherwise.

"So it is my mission to make him happy?"

"If you wish to accept it?"

"You failed to add, 'Mr. Phelps'."

"Mr. Phelps."

"Only, here, if I don't accept my impossible missions, I just become stuck here."

"You just used 'here' twice in that sentence, it's not very good English."

"Why have you decided to irritate me?"

"The term that I would have preferred, would be distract."

"You don't need to distract me, I'm perfectly okay."

"Is that why your heart is beating so fast?"

Faron refocuses his attention on his little Asiatic body, the heart is truly beating much quicker than it should, his breathing is also quicker and shallower than it might be.

However, he does not choose to acknowledge this and moves the conversation forwards.

"Why am I here?"

"Now that is a deep, philosophical question. It is certainly a novel way to keep us distracted while we wait."

They arrive at the docks. It is even darker and more dangerous seeming than walking through the village.

Piles of crates are stacked up, in twos, threes, fours and more, but without any clear logic as to how or why they are where they are.

Sailors and porters of many nations hang around, sitting, standing, even laying down, but without any clear logic as to how or why they are where they are.

The atmosphere is menacing and chaotic, but the guide didn't seem at all concerned.

Maybe he is just more aware that this is just a manifestation of Faron's imagination, and nothing really bad can possibly happen.

After all, it isn't, in any important manner, real.

"No, I don't mean, 'why am I here?' I mean, 'why is Faron here?'"

"Exactly, very astute nuance. Because, you are not Faron, you are Fukuchō."

"That's right."

"So the question could be asked otherwise, why is Faron here, sharing Fukuchō's body?"

"No, no, that's not at all what I wanted to ask. Why is Faron, Father Fróis, here?"

"Because he is supposed to be."

"That is not a real answer."

"Everyone that is here, is here for a purpose."

"Well none of them are happy. He isn't happy, my mother does not seem very happy either. Nor does Madeleine either, actually, nobody seems very happy."

"Then you certainly will have many people that you can help."

"I'm supposed to make them all happy…"

"If that was supposed to be a question, then it is also its own response."

They are walking slowly to the jetty and they watch a big ship come into the docks.

Many of the sailors and dock hands, suddenly spring into action to catch and secure the lines of ropes, thrown over from the side of the ship.

Silently they watch as the whole dock seems to come to life and a multi-coloured stream of humanity, and some animals, disembark from the bowels of this vast wooden arc.

"And the priest, is it also my job is to help him to find pleasure?"

"Why not?"

And with that, they lapse once again into a thoughtful silence, waiting for the young man to appear.

It seems everyone has left the boat and they start to eye each other, wondering who would be first to question if he is really coming or not.

Then, finally, the young man comes out for the ship. Small and fragile looking, he wears a long, heavy coat and an Irish looking cap.

He walks slowly down the ramp, as if he is fighting within himself, as to whether to leave the ship at all.

Being in the same body, it is impossible to know if it is Faron or Fukuchō that is reacting, but the sight of this family member, sends a… thunder bolt of emotions, into and through it.

Somewhere, it isn't such a real surprise to see that it is none other than Jay, but his reaction is still very confused and mixed and when Jay approaches them he does not move for a few seconds.

… Until the training of the body take over, Fukuchō makes a quite slow and long bow.

"Welcome to Japan, honoured guest."

Jay hesitates for a moment, then his lips tighten and twist. His pupils seem to totally disappear.

"You have the same eyes and nose as me. You must be my cousin, my mother died because of your mother."

"How do you know that?" Simple question.

"I got a letter from the Jesuit priest."

"Why would he do that?" Confusion.

"Because someone needs to tell the truth."

"But it wasn't her fault." Panic, need to defend.

"Are you saying that the priest lied?"

"But it wasn't like that." Pleading

"And how old were you at the time?"

"I was seven." Simple fact.

"And I was five."

She turns to the monk, a certain panic in her voice. "Can't the Daimyo gets another interpreter? Can't you do it?"

"This is something that you have to do, my child, this is your Karma."

"But he hates me."

"And talking about me in the third person, while I'm standing here, is not very polite."

The reference to politeness, strikes Fukuchō, in her Achilles' heel.

"Mr. Pinkerton-sama, I am most sorry, please accept my most humble apologies…" She is now, really panicking, talking and bowing, and bowing and talking.

"… It was most rude of me. Please, please, please do not take offence. I was shocked and surprised to see you, after so long. I am sorry that you believe that my mother was the cause of your mother's death. It was a shock for all of us. Please, Mr. Pinkerton-sama, please, please forgive me."

"Mr. Pinkerton, could you please at least say that you accept her apology for being rude, or else we could be here all night."

The tone and the content takes a moment to succeed to enter into the tortured consciousness of the visitor, but when it finally manages to break through into his thought process, he suddenly sees just how ridiculous the scene must seem.

"If I say that I accept your apology, will you stop talking and bowing?"

"You will forgive me?" She is desperate.

"Fine, I forgive you for being rude."

"Thank you, thank you, Mr. Pinkerton-sama …"

"Could you now please stop talking and bowing?"

If anything, it was Faron's influence that finally succeeded to cool the panic of the young Geisha trainee.

"And you are?"

"Brother Jakuren, at your service."

"Then permit me to introduce myself, for I also have forgotten my manners: My name is, Benjamin Dole Pinkerton, and I am the son of …"

"…Lieutenant Benjamin Franklin Pinkerton, and Madame Butterfly," the guide completed. "You are known throughout the region, as much for your father, as for your mother."

"So I am to be a person of interest, an exhibit in my own freak show."

"Your father was most respected and appreciated by all, especially his excellence Shimazu Yoshihisa the Daimyo.*

"And my crazy mother?"

"Your mother was not crazy."

"Well she killed herself, didn't she?"

"Ritual suicide, seppuku, is an honourable death. Your mother was of a respected samurai family, it was her right to end her life in that manner. There is no dishonour on her or on you, rising from this act."

"I don't understand, she killed herself, only crazy people do that."

"Not in Japan."

"I came back to try and understand what happened."

"Then, son, open yourself to all the possible truths."

"What does that mean?"

"Jūnin toiro, ten persons, ten colours, ten persons, ten truths."

"That each person has their own version of the truth?"

"You are here to learn."

"But where is the truth to be found?"

"Finally, once you have given ear to each and every truth, then, and only then can you seek it at its source."

"And where might that be?"

"In your own heart."

"I would deign to follow your wise words, old man, but alas, I cannot, for my heart is broken and none of your sage advice can change that."

"What is wrong, child?" Again there are feelings of shame and guilt, wracking the little, frail body.

"Please excuse me venerable one I have shamed myself I have thought to question this the decision of my Daimyo. He ordered me to accompany my cousin, and I have thought to question his command."

Fukuchō lowers her head in shame, and waits. Everything stops, Jay shows signs of being very uncomfortable, but he hardly moves, nor does he say a word.

The monk gently lifts up her head.

"Do not worry my child no one will ever hear about this." And he turns and looks pointedly at Jay.

"How can I tell anyone? Almost no one speaks English."

"Fine, shall we go then?"

The relief is not total, she has been too well brought up to allow herself, to be let off the hook so easily, but there are other things to do, and it is getting very late.

"Where can I take you to, Mr. Benjamin Dole Pinkerton-sama?"

"You can please take me to me mother's house. And you can also stop with the crazy titles, everyone calls me Benji, please could you address me as such."

"Yes, Benji-sama."

"What is this 'sama'?"

“It means something like ‘sir’.”

“Well, you can forget that as well, just Benji, will do fine.”

“Yes Benji-sama, sorry, yes Benji.” She bows, he shakes his head, they turn, and the guide lights the path.

“I suppose that it won’t be much more than a ruin.”

“Oh no, it has always been looked after. It is the pride of our family that it has never been left to decay.

And when he heard of your coming, the Daimyo ordered that it be cleaned and prepared for you, if you should wish to stay there.”

“Your family have looked after it.”

“It is our duty and our pleasure.”

"Oh," was all he could think, or allow himself to reply.

They carry on in silence, each in their own separate, yet intrinsically linked worlds.

7. An unfortunate meeting

Being lower
Then a samurai,
Easy, headless.

They are walking in silence back through the village. They will soon turn off, and take one of the small, costal paths, towards the secluded residence, of the famous Madame Butterfly.

Coming from the other direction is a heavy set young man, he is wearing a sleeveless jacket with extensive shoulders, wide, flowing trousers, with a long sword and a short sword, tucked into his ribbon, belt.

He walks in a slightly, heavy, clumsy seeming fashion, he is not bothering to carry a torch.

To begin with, it is not possible to see his face, but both the guide and Fukuchō must recognise him, as they exchange glances as he comes into view.

Faron realises this, but has a great deal of trouble reading Fukuchō's reactions to the man. Fear, respect, excitement, desire, pleasure, anger and disappointment spin round and round her confused system.

Emotional bullets, in a six shot, revolver, playing a mad game of Russian roulette.

He approaches closer, another of the known actors, makes his entrance, this time it's Mike.

"Konbanwa, Hattori Hanzō-San," and she bows, quite low.

"Konbanwa, Fukuchō-San," and he nods, slightly. He then turns to the monk, who politely inclines.

"Jakuren-San."

"Hattori-San."

He then stops, his gaze slides over to Jay.
Jay looks back at him, but does not move.

The silence begins to stretch. Seconds are
slowly, slowly passing by; like a lazy
herd of elephants, heavy and laborious,
returning home after a full days toil.

Mike seems to be being very calm,
patiently waiting for something to
happen, but nothing does.

Faron is highly aware that Fukuchō, who
has since straightened up, is unusually,
tense.

Why her energetic bowstring have
become so stretched, he just cannot
imagine, but no cat, waiting for a mouse,
to emerge from its hole, was ever more
ready.

The movement is almost unperceivable,
an ever so slight exhale.
'So that is the way it has to be'.
Then the pupils, constrict.
'I line up the target'.
Finally, a slight twitch of the upper
muscles of the right arm.
'Prepare for the gesture'.

She knows what is coming.
She is Japanese, she has seen this, so
many times before.
She knows that he has every right to.
She understands that he obliged to.
She sees it coming.
It is execution.
It is DEATH.

The panic and fear pass as a flash of
sunlight reflected on an opening window.
Faron, has no time to integrate the act.
She turns, bends and hits Jay solidly
across his midriff, with all the power that
can be channelled into the side of her thin
arm.

Jay doubles over in shock, surprise and pain.

"What the …?" He never gets to finish the phrase, because he is struck by a second, even more violent surprise.

The long sword of the man, has just skimmed across the top of his head. Only a split second before, where his neck had been.

"You are supposed to bow," Faron heard himself explain, to the stunned cousin, nursing his aching stomach, too scared to move, even the slightest inch.

The man looks down at the panicked youth, gives a quick nod, then turns his attention to Fukuchō.

"So you haven't forgotten everything?"

"I have forgotten nothing. One day, I'll beat you again."

"You are a woman, that day will never dawn. Good-night." And, with another slight bow, he turns and resumes his passage into the dark night.

"You can get up now," the monk bends down and helps him back to his feet.

He glares at Fukuchō.

"Is that the way that you are educated to treat your guests? Punch them in the guts?

Even if you hate me for telling the truth about your mother, that still doesn't excuse you for what you've done.

I'm going to make sure that everyone hears about this."

She stops for a moment, again the panic of having acted in an inappropriate way.

"She has just saved your life," he informs him, in a simple, matter of fact voice.

Jay goes very quiet for a moment.

"Are you serious?"

"Very serious, I'm afraid. You failed to bow to a Samurai."

"And that gives him the right to cut my head off?"

"No, not the right, …., the obligation. The rules of conduct and right behaviour are everything, here in Japan.

If you fail to follow the social rules, then, even as an honoured guest, you can still end up at the end of someone's sword."

"Then it is your responsibility to show me, to explain these things to me."

"There wasn't time, I am very sorry Benji-san, it was again my fault. I had to strike you to save your life, but it is also an unforgivable act.

Again I must ask for your forgiveness, a forgiveness that I know that I do not deserve."

And then she stops, and she bows, and in a solitary, secluded, silence, she stands and awaits, her sentence.

Jay also stops for a moment, "she saved my life?"

"To have been able to react as quickly as a Samurai, is a very rare thing to see. If you would have been with anyone else, we wouldn't be having this conversation, at least, not in this world."

"Then I was lucky to have had you as my interpreter," he gently takes her hands and raises her up.

She slowly, straightens up, and they stop. For the first time they take a moment to look into each other's eyes.

"I feel like I know you."

"Of course you know me, Benji-san, you are my little cousin Ben."

"I'm not following you."

"When and where do you think that I learned to speak English?" He shrugs
.
"When playing with you, Father Fróis would bring me to your house. We would play together, and he would talk to us in English, and teach us to read the English Bible."

"You were my play friend, with the pigtails that I would pull?"

"You remember me."

"But it's not possible, your mother hated my mother, why would she let you to come a play with me, and learn English with me?"

"Here we are." They have arrived at the small, doll-like house of Butterfly.

Jay's attention slips out of the knotty question of his mother's and aunt's relationship, and focusses itself on the house of his earliest childhood memories, and most awful day of his entire life.

"Where did she do it?"

"Do you really want to know?" Responded the monk.

"Yes, yes I do."

"In here," Jay follows him into the house and they walk into the centre of the main room.

Jay then suddenly turns, "GET OUT, GET OUT!"

She is shocked and surprised, but the
monk only gently takes her by the hand,
and leads her out, out of the house, and
into the courtyard, out into dark, deep
night.

Out, into the dead of night.

8. A Morning Meeting

A rainbow
Of food, paints
The palette.

Faron is approaching the doll house. He
has been up for some time, as the
preparations to leave, not forgetting the
full white face makeup, takes some
doing.

In passing, he has gulped down
something that passes as breakfast; some
freshly boiled white rice rolled up in a
sheet of dried seaweed called nori, and
dipped in soy sauce.

He has a message to deliver, which was
waiting for him when he got home, last
night;

'The honoured guest, Benjamin Dole
Pinkerton, has been invited to present
himself before the Daimyo, at eleven
o'clock in the morning'.

79

He slips off his sandals and walks into the house. Before the sliding door, leading to the main room, he kneels down and opens it gently.

Jay is sitting, slightly uncomfortably on the floor, or to be correct, on a tatami.

In front of him is a complete breakfast tray. Faron didn't have time to see what is on it, before he finds himself in a deep bow.

Jay must have hear the door sliding and he must have noticed the visitor.

"Who is it?"

"Ohayō gozaimasu, Benji-san".

"What?"

"Good morning, Benji-san."

"Fine, good morning. …. Why are you staying there, bowing?"

"I must wait for you to invite me into your room."

"Okay, then come in. …What are you doing now?"

"One always comes into a room on one's knees, it is a mark of respect."

"Oh, okay... Is this normal?" He points to the breakfast tray.

On it is a bowl of white rice, a bowl of soup, some pickled vegetables, some pieces of nori, grilled fish, and some natto.

"Yes, it is a bit more than I have for breakfast, but much, much less than the Daimyo eats."

"I don't even know what all of this is."

"So, this is white rice …"

"That I have worked out for myself …"

"This is osumashi, clear soup, pickled vegetables, these are dried nori, seaweed, grilled fish, these are called natto, fermented soy beans."

Benji, digs his chopsticks into the bean bowl.

"It looks disgusting."

"They are very healthy, and although they are a bit sticky, they are very good to eat. If you prefer, you can just add some to the soup."

"I'll think to pass on that. … Why are you here, now?"

"Oh, yes, you are summoned to come, this morning to present yourself in front of Shimazu Yoshihisa, the Daimyo."

"What's a Daimyo?"

"In your language, I was told that it means feudal lord. He owns this whole province. It seems that he very much appreciated your father."

"Yeh, well, it seems that lots of people seemed to appreciate him."

"You didn't?"

"Not that it's any business of yours, but he was rarely with us, and even when he was, he was often in a bad humour, and mostly, more than a little drunk."

"He wasn't a happy man?"

"I don't think that I ever saw him happy. Maybe he was guilty about the death of my mother, it was also his fault.

I think that she must have loved him, and when he can back with Kate, and said that he was taking me away with him.

Well, it just seems that maybe he must have felt a bit guilty.”

“Maybe he also loved her.”

Benji turns angrily towards her. “Don’t make me laugh. If he had loved her, he would never have left Japan the first time.

He would never had married Kate. He would not have come back to get me, and even then, he would have seen her and stayed.

Don’t talk such bulge, he never loved her, my father never loved my mother, not ever!”

“I’m sorry, I’m just so sorry. I shouldn’t have spoken, it wasn’t my place, I’m sorry, I’m sorry.”

“Oh my God, don’t start all this bowing stuff again. I just can’t stand it. Get out, go and wait for me outside, I’ll finish some of this stuff.”

Faron, who has been taking a back seat in all this, is once again surprised, as, seemingly totally out of the blue, she turns back to Jay.

"If you roll the rice in the nori, the seaweed, and then dip it into the soup, it's really nice like that." And before he has the chance to reply, she has shuffled out of the room.

Now that she is outside, Faron directs her towards the cliffs, overlooking the magnificent sea view.

With a certain soothing energy, which he has until then, been unaware of, he succeeds to quieten down her waves of panic and remorse.

It also gives him time to reflect on his own reactions to his ostracised, younger brother.

Here he is, in a story, created just for him, about people, that seem to have done awful things to each other, full of secrets and possibly lies.

Each is harbouring, deep seated pain and suffering. What it is in their pasts that has created such emotional torture, is as yet still a mystery to him, and will possibly remain as such.

What is clear, is that these are not bad people, they have surly done what they had thought that they had to.

So, are they really at fault, for what they have or have not; done, said, thought?

Maybe it wouldn't be so wrong, to accept that Jean-Jacques, Jay, had acted the only way that he could, and that he wasn't the awful traitor that Faron had chosen to see him as.

'Oh Jay, Jay, why have I forsaken, thee?'

But before he could continue his soliloquy, someone enters into a dialogue.

"So, let's go a see this lord, shall we?"

9. An Audience with the Daimyo

"You don't like me much, either, do you?"

"You are an honoured guest of the Daimyo, and I am your interpreter."

"Listen, whatever your name is, what is your name anyway?"

"It's Fukuchō."

"Fookoo-what?"

"Fukuchō, it means 'fortunate butterfly'."

"Butterfly? Like my mother?"

"Only also lucky."

"Yeh, she wasn't very lucky, my mother."

"She was a nice person."

"You remember her?"

"Of course, she was my aunt, I played with you, often, since I was about three, or so I understand."

"So why do you hate me?"

"I don't hate you."

"Come on, it's not only because your mother didn't help mine, and you know that, that you react like you do to me."

Faron is troubled, is his negative reactions to Jay, (hey, he thinks of him as Jay, again), that have affected Fukucho's reactions towards Benji?

"You want me to be honest?"

"Yes, I want you to be honest."

"Your mother stole your father from my mother, he was with her first."

"That's not true."

"And when she committed seppuku, my mother became very, very sad, and stayed sad for many years.

Seppuku is an honourable act, and as such cannot be questioned, but the effect on my mother was very strong, and maybe I blame her. So also maybe, I am blaming you."

"So you are angry with me because your mother was depressed after my mother committed suicide, and I am angry with you, because your mother didn't stop her committing suicide."

"Yes, that would seem to be about it."

Benji thrusts his hands into the oversize pockets of his western, pinstriped trousers, and walks a while in silence.

Fukucho, used to the practice of silence, walks respectfully, along beside him.

"It doesn't really make much sense for us to be angry with other. And I feel something very comfortable being with you. I suppose that you are the closest thing to family that I have."

"We are first cousins."

"Then how about we start acting like cousins?"

"No."

"No?"

"No, let us get back to being cousins."

"Hi c'us."

"Hi to you too cousin." And she starts to
cry.

Faron can feel an enormous sense of
release and relief flowing through her. As
well as joy and caring.

However, the fashion that this female self
finds to express this, is, through tears.

The tears come from a deep, lost well,
hidden in the most profound and
protected parts of her person.

The loss of Benji had been horribly
difficult to bear. If she wouldn't have had
Hattori, as her other boy friend, playmate, she wouldn't have been able to
carry on.

Having him come back, and feeling the
animosity between the two of them, was
just like turning the knife, in an old and
painful wound.

Now, now that he was really back, was
one of the greatest presents in the world
for her.

And so, there was nothing else to do, but
to open up the floodgates, and to cry.

Benji doesn't quite know what to do, so
like the good man that he is, he just
continues to walk, quietly beside her, and
hopes that it will end soon. –
Which it does.

Feeling much more comfortable with
each other, they arrive at the Daimyo's
palace.

They are politely welcomed into the
palace and led to the door leading into the
great hall.

Fukucho is about to enter shuffling on her
knees, but is quietly instructed to walk up
to the point where the line of the other
invitees ends. It is at that point that they
should stop, stop and bow.

She tries to explain this to Benji, but he doesn't really capture what she is trying to explain.

"Just follow my lead, when I stop, you stop, when I bow, you bow."

"Okay".

"You will bow this time, won't you?"

"This guy is a lord, that other was just an upstart, hardly older than we are."

"Hattori Hanzō, is a little older than my age, but he is a Samurai, so you need to bow to him, or he can legally, chop you head off."

"Then let's hope that we don't meet him again."

At this point, they are interrupted by the door being opened for them.

The great hall is quite full of people, both men and women. They are all kneeling row upon row, facing the great man.

He is comfortably relaxing on a small cushion, placed on the tatami, and is gently fanning himself.

They walk respectfully along the passage between the rows of people, until they reach the last of the rows, where Fukuchō comes to a halt.

Benji, totally attentive to her, stops also. She immediately drops into a full bow, knees bent, head to the floor.

He can see that the Daimyo has noticed them and follows her, but in a western type, deep bow.

"Come, come, both of you, come here to me." Benji looks to Fukuchō to confirm what he has understood.

She gets back to her feet, (feeling a little uncomfortable), and gestures for Benji to advance towards the mats.

A cushion appears immediately by the side of the master, and Jay takes it. He does his best to kneel down as the others do.

Fukucho, knees down close to him, close enough to whisper into his ear, she translates the greeting.

"Mr. Benjamin Dole Pinkerton son of Lieutenant Benjamin Franklin Pinkerton and Madame Butterfly, of the Inaba clan, you honour us with your presence.

From this moment you are the special guest of Shimazu Yoshihisa, Daimyo of this province.

Benji, turns to Fukucho. "Please tell that I very much appreciate his welcome." But before Fukucho is able to begin to speak.

"That won't be necessary, I will translate for you, it is more fitting that it is a man that would fulfil such duties." It is Faron, or to be more exact, it is Faron, Father Luís Fróis.

"I would very much appreciate that. Are you Father Fróis?"

"Yes I am," he inclines his head, as a form of curtesy bow, and then turns to the Daimyo, to translate.

He thanks the lord in Benji's name. The Daimyo bows in acknowledgement, and then continues.

"As the last male of the noble clan of Inaba, it is necessary that you take on the honour of your family."

He makes a slight gesture to someone behind him, and the retainers bring forward; a suit of light armour, a helmet, and two swords, one long, one short.

"I have been holding on to these since the death of your grandfather, and now they are to be passed to you."

Suddenly someone stands up, everyone looks round. The person hurries to the centre isle and prostrates himself in from of his master.

"What is it, Hattori-san?" Shimazu, is a slightly vexed to be interrupted at this moment.

"Master, if I may speak?"

"Please do."

"Is not against tradition to give them to him? Only samurai can wear the daisho: it represents the social power and personal honour of the samurai."

Shimazu, stops for a moment; as a noble and as a Japanese, but mostly as the Daimyo, he has long learned to keep his face inscrutable, unreadable.

The eyes, however, are a different matter;
first the eyes fix on Mike, the gaze is hard
and the pupils shrink into mean, little
darts of hostility.

However, one does not get to the level of
power and privilege, such as he has,
without being able to outmanoeuvre a
smart-arse child.

The eyes then dilate and float up and
right and then left, and then right again.

Finally, the eyes find back their twinkle,
and just the merest of smiles strokes the
old man's lips, before being deftly wiped
away, with the flick of his fan.

"Thank you, Hattori, you are of course
totally correct, the swords of a samurai
can only be given to a samurai. Hence, I
declare this now to be a kakan ceremony,
I will bestow on our kinsman, his new
curtesy name, of, of, Zǐchǎn."

"Come here Benjamin Pinkerton." He gets up, slightly confused, Fukucho has not been able to explain all that is being said.

"Benjamin, you are to go and kneel before the Daimyo, he going to, to knight you."

"To knight me?"

"That, I believe is the correct English term, hurry lad, everyone is waiting."

"As Daimyo of this province, I proclaim that your new curtesy name is Zǐchǎn, and that you have officially come of age, and that I bestow on you the rank, honour and title of samurai."

"Maybe it would be polite to thank him?" The remarks, with a slight smile.

"How do you say thank you?"

"Doumo arigatou gozaimasu"

"Doomo arigatoo gozamasoo". J.J. stops for a moment, then bursts out laughing.

"Yokatta, yokatta‼"

"I think that he appreciates your efforts."

"What do I do now?"

"I would suggest that you wait for him to continue."

Shimazu, turns and takes the long sword from the functionary, and solemnly passes it horizontally to Jay, who takes it carefully with both hands.

"That sword is called a katana and it is the sword of a samurai, you must never be without it, and that short sword, is called a wakizash and together they are referred to as the daisho."

"Why is he doing this?"

"I will try to explain later, but he hadn't planned to do this, this is how he is saving his own face."

The ceremony finally comes to a close and Jay leaves the castle with a borrowed obi belt, sash, with, uncomfortably, crossed within it, his two new swords.

"I'm supposed to get to wear these all the time?"

"It is a very great honour that you have had bestowed on you, this day, Benji-sama"

"The priest said that he had been somehow forced to make me a samurai today, why?"

"He was giving you the swords and armour of your grandfather, our grandfather. Oh, something important, nobody is know that we are cousins, that I am the daughter of my mother.

Everybody thinks that I am an orphan."

"Are you going to explain that to me?"

"Not now, here in the street, someone might pass that has learned enough English to understand."

"Okay, you were saying about the swords."

"And Hattori said ..."

"Someone taking my name in vain?"

"You only know enough of the bible to use it for your own conceit."

"You never did have much sense of humour." He then turns to Benji. "Yoi tsuitachi, Zǐchǎn." And he bows politely.

"You should say, 'Yoi tsuitachi, Hattori', and bow."

"I will not bow to him."

"But it is not polite."

"I am now a samurai, he cannot make me."

"He cannot make you, but it would be impolite." Benji turns, smiles at Hattori, but does not bow.

"Fine, your samurai boyfriend, has not chosen to be respectful to me, so I challenge him to Kettō."

"Kettō? You cannot be serious, he doesn't know how to fight, how can he meet you in a duel?"

"He will be in the field, behind the old school at eight o'clock tomorrow morning or he will be deemed a coward and then be obliged to commit seppuku, for his shame."

"Why are you doing this? He has done nothing to you?"

"He has insulted me twice, once was more than enough."

"What's going on now? Why doesn't that oaf just leave us alone?"

"Because he has just challenged you to a duel."

"A duel, what sort of a duel?"

"A samurai duel, using those swords, possibly to the death."

"You are joking, of course."

"Does he look like he's joking?"

"But he can't do that, I'm an honoured guest. It would be, it would be, be, impolite. That's it, it would be impolite, so he can't do it."

"It was you, Benjamin, that has been impolite. He came, wished you good afternoon and bowed, you refused to return his salutation, nor did you bow."

"Well it's not enough to force me to duel with him, I'll just go and see that big boss, and get him to tell him off for being unpleasant with his guest."

"Benji, you are now a samurai, you are bound by the rules and customs of the samurai, there is no one that can change that."

"And if I refuse to fight, then you will be branded as a coward …"

"I've had worse …"

"And be forced to commit ritual suicide in front of the whole village."

"You cannot be serious."

"This is very serious Benji-san."

"But what am I to do?"

"You can try and be polite now, perhaps
he will accept your apology."

Jay turns very slowly towards Mike.
"Good afternoon, Hattori'-san," and
bows, quite deeply.

"Sayōnara, Zǐchǎn-san. Eight o'clock,
don't let him be late." He bows to both of
them, and leaves.

"So, how did I do?"

"Not quite good enough."

"But what can we do?"

"I will make you tea. Making tea is a
good way to find answers for things."

"How is that?"

"The tea ceremony is an ancient ritual, it
purifies the soul and quietens the mind."

10. Time for Tea

Only the
Clearest of waters
For green tea.

The birds sing,
The well of purest water,
The ladle is taken, wiped and thanked.

The water sparkles,
It is drawn with respect,
Hands, face, feet, paths are washed.

Cha no Yu begins,
Enter the room on knees,
All that is required, is already in place.

The kettle boils,
Carry the tray to the kettle,
The waste water bowl, bring separately.

Move it forward,
Pull out the fukusa cloth,
From the wide obi sash, briskly.

Take the cloth,
Pull it taught, snap,
Crease it, with a hand chop, fold.

Clean the natsume
This thin, lacquered box,
Hiding, green, powdered, treasure.

Take the cloth,
Pull it taught, snap,
Crease it, with a hand chop, fold.

Clean chashaku
Tea ladle of bamboo
With three wipes of fukusa soft.

Take the chasen out
Tea whisk from its bowl
To then stand it on the tray.

Put down fukusa,
Take out linen chakin, cloth
To clean the tea bowl, chawan.

Thrice round the rim,
And three times, then within,
Then separately, on the tray with them.

Then with water hot,
Fill the chawan, not quite full,
Then clink the chasen, into the bowl.

Then pick it up,
And rotate the brush,
Then clink, again and whisk.

Remove the chasen,
And back onto the tray,
Then dump the water, away.

Take the chashaku,
And then the natsume,
Take off the lid, place on try.

Take the chashaku,
Two scoops of matcha,
Place them in the tea bowl.

Clink chashaku,
The lid is back on,
They return to the tray.

Take the fukusa,
Pour hot water into bowl,
Whisk slowly, and then quickly.

The tea froths,
Remove the chasen,
Place it back, onto the tray.

Take the bowl,
Turn twice clockwise,
Serve to guest, and bow.

Guest raises bowl, and bows,
Turn twice clockwise,
Then ready.

Guest drinks tea, in three sips,
Slurp last sip, tea is,
Really good.

The empty bowl is taken,
Again, hot water,
Rotate bowl.

Dump the water out,
More hot water,
Whisk shortly.

Dump the water out,
Chakin, in bowl,
And chasen.

Fold again the fukusa,
Re -clean chashaku,
Place on bowl.

Move the natsume to the right,
Pat fukusa, twice,
Put it away.

The tea ceremony is now complete.

11.Celebration

**A bowl of sake
Open your mouth
Open your soul.**

"We should celebrate."

"What, my imminent doom."

"Sorry, I don't understand."

"Are we to celebrate my being hacked to death by your childhood friend?"

"I was more thinking about celebrating your being made a samurai, and that I think that maybe I might have an idea."

"You have an idea about how I can get out of this?"

"Maybe."

"So what is it?"

"I'll tell you when it is time."

"And that's it? I just have to trust that it will be okay?"

"You will just have to trust me."

 "I suppose that I don't have much of anyone else."

"So, I'll go and heat some sake."

"That's alcohol?"

"Yes."

"And it's drunk hot?"

"Warm."

"Like English beer?"

"What is English beer?"

"Never mind."

"Come sit."

"Is that a tea pot?"

"This is for the sake."

"And exactly what is sake?"

"Sake, can just mean alcoholic drink, but it also means rice wine."

"And it is always served hot?"

"No, this is Junshu sake, it is a traditional type of sake that's rich and dense; it can be served warm or hot."

"Not bad, not bad at all."

"Now I have something else for you to taste."

"What is it?"

"It is called mugijōchū, it is made from mugi. From cereals, barley, barley shōchū."

"Sure, I'll give it a try. What? This, this is like whisky, and not a bad whisky, at that."

"To my cousin."

"To my cousin, beautiful and smart."

"Handsome, and brave."

"You know I came here, I came here, because I didn't have anywhere else to go."

"Now you have come home, let's drink to your coming home."

"I thought about jumping off of the, the ship."

"I don't understand."

"I thought about killing myself. I was not
very happy. You see, Kate, well Kate was
a bit of a bitch.

You, you see, she married dad because he
was a lieutenant, he was a lieutenant and
has father was a general. He was
handsome and he was a good catch.

He married her, 'cus he thought that his
father would be proud that he married
someone from a good family, even if they
were poor. Dad spent the whole of his
life trying to get his father's approval.

Kate, yes, Kate was a bitch. She was
always trying to get me to behave, what
does that mean, to behave? I've never
worked it out.

So, she wasn't happy, because dad must
have felt guilty about mum, about
Butterfly, even though he never spoke
about her. And I sure as hell wasn't
allowed to, iether, either, iether, either,
what-ever.

Let's have another drink."

She pours him more shōchū.

"Dad, nobody let me call him dad. He was just never there, either he was away on his ship, or he was away, in his bottle.

God did that man know how to drink. To captain his ship and to drink himself stupid, that's what was good to do.

Well, I'm going to get myself killed tomorrow, and frankly I don't really care. I've nothing what-so-ever to live for, so let's have another drink."

And so they do, and so they did.

12. The Ace of Swords

The field is dry, the vampire sun has
sucked the life out of the blood grass,
now laying, limp and lifeless.

Hattori Hanzō, in full ceremonial armour;
is already there waiting, savouring his
victory, in the early, listless, morning sun.

Whether his opponent will appear or not,
either way, victory will be his.

This, for the attentive spectator, might be
well possible to perceive, the attentive
spectator being the second combatant
who is just arriving.

Hattori, from the change in his posture,
shows a certain surprise to see that his
opponent has dared to appear, the two
suited fighters approach.

In truth, he is quite a bit surprised to find himself here, but, for good or for bad, somewhere, he has no choice but to face the samurai.

The dried, bloody tips of the grass, dance gloomily in the morning breeze. Whispering a last; lingering, liturgy for the life of the lost soul, about to be liberated and led towards the eternal light.

He has a little trouble with the suit of armour, which he dons for the very first time, this morning.

Hattori advances several more steps, then stops, at the appropriate distance, bows and waits.

He doesn't have to wait for long, for, in correct manner, his opponent looks straight towards him, and effects the same curtesy bow.

The slanted brown eyes and outline of a
slightly beakish nose are all he can see,
but something about the regard is
disconcerting.

In place of the fear that he has expected,
there is a fierce look of anger, even
hatred, reflecting back at him.

He repeats the unfamiliar terms; the
Tsuka, the sword handle, gripped tightly,
too tightly in his right hand.

The saya, the scabbard, held ready in his
left, ready to anchor it, when time to draw
the blade, the nakago.

Time stops, both protagonists face each
other. He continues to grip the hilt of the
long, curved sword, vaguely asking
himself, why the hell he is here, now,
facing this dealer of death.

Suddenly the dark, dream begins;

Hattori takes a half step back, the sword,
slides, smooth and silent from its sheath.

It hovers; a micro moment above his
head, left hand contacts the hilt.

The wicked blade sweeps down,
delivering death.

To the head, helmet or none.

But no.

His body now knows.

His arm twitches, and

The blade appears.

And flows,

Upwards.

The swords meet,

The descent is deflected,

And slides,

Along the other's side.

He absorbs the blow,

Although smaller,

And lighter than the other.

The blades,

Disengage.

And he takes the opportunity

To strike.

Hattori,
Momentarily disoriented,

Reacts instinctively,

Deflects the blade

With his armoured wrist.

Then doubles his efforts,

He retreats.

Stops.

Sword stopped,

Points heavenwards.

Steps forwards,

Slashes towards,

The West.

The left side,

Less guarded,

More vulnerable,

Offers an attractive

Target.

But not

Fast enough.

The parry,

Arrives.

But that too is

Expected.

Slice to the East.

The response is

Fractionally

Slow.

Ahhhh,

The Pain.

It cuts

Through his

Senses.

Pain

Weakens

The spirit.

And slows

The reflexes.

A cut North-West,

Parry,

But only just

The world

Swims,

The next

Will be,

The last.

"Yamete!" Hattori, educated, as all
Japanese, heeds the command to stop.

He turns from his prey, and is shocked to
see Father Fróis, who had called out,
accompanied by, Mr Benjamin Dole
Zĭchăn Pinkerton.

He bends down and grabs the helmet of
the warrior, who he was at the point of
dispatching.

"You!"

Faron looks up at the blazing eyes of
Mike, he thanks all the stars that the other
Faron has arrived before he could be
further wounded.

He is still confused just how, Fukuchō, could force him to have done all that she had gotten him to do, since yesterday afternoon.

He still has no idea, what would happen to him, if he was mortally wounded during one of these incarnations.

"You? How dare you? Taking on the armour of a samurai, being in public without being properly attired for the maiko that you are. The shame, the shame."

Suddenly, Faron finds himself full of rage, Fukuchō springs onto her feet.

"I should have shame? And you, you have no shame for what you have done?"

"And exactly what have I done to be ashamed of?"

"All of this. To have manoeuvred Benji-san into a situation where you could challenge him to a Kettō, full knowing that he could neither defend himself, nor find someone to defend him.

Then, you arrive here without a witness, nor an interpreter so that he can hear and accept your challenge.

And worse than that, you didn't even present yourself, by name and the names of your ancestors, nor of your Sensei."

"Is this so?"

Before Faron has time to ask himself, what in Heaven's name Duncan is doing there. Mike is already humbling himself before him.

"Konnichiwa otousan," bowing deeply.

'Good-day father?'

'Oh my God, Duncan is his father', then, as if watching a speeded up video, images upon images flash through his consciousness.

Miyamoto, for that is his name, seeming huge, inviting her into his house. Meeting the child Mike, Hattori, her new playmate.

Hours and hours of playing together, playing many games, fighting with sticks.

Then Miyamoto, solemnly informing them that Hattori is to begin his training to fight, and that Fukuchō will be his training partner.

And then hours and hours of practicing, and all laughing, and pushing, and then, and then, the kiss.

And then it ended; no more fighting, or pushing, or talking or even being invited to their house, even if it was almost next door.

"What is this nonsense? What of your honour?"

"What my honour? What of her honour? A nobody, without even a family name, wearing samurai armour, wielding a katana."

"She is not a nobody."

"Well that is what you called her. Daughter of who knows which Geisha, and who knows what drunken sailor.

Someone with no name, some who could never marry into any decent family.

That's what you said." He then turns to growl at Fukuchō.

"Well now, you have found someone that will have you. Someone who has no honour to uphold, I hope that you will both be happy."

Duncan, Miyamoto Hanzō, seems very taken aback. He turns and speaks quietly to his son.

"The sword is to be used only in the spirit of gokoku taihei: to 'defend the great peace.' It is not for dispatching vermin that irritate you."

And with that he turns, throwing an imperial glance at Mike, who sheaths his katana, throws one last dart of hatred at Faron, and hurries to leave with his older.

"Why did you do that? You got me drunk last night. Father Fróis has tried to explain, but I couldn't keep up. I just don't understand anything."

"Come let us go and have some breakfast, and then I would for us to take a bath."

"What together?"

"It is a custom here, it is normal for friends to bath together."

He turns to the father for clarification.

"Yes, it is a normal Japanese custom, most respectable."

"Father?"

"Yes, my child?"

"Thank you."

"For what?"

"For coming, for saving my life."

"There is no need to thank me for that, it is part of my duties."

"Thank you, just the same."

"It is a brave and generous woman that would take the place of another in such circumstances."

"He's my little cousin, I couldn't have done otherwise."

"Many would have done otherwise,
believe me. Now, I think that my work is
done here for the moment.

And I will bid you both a beautiful day.
And, enjoy your bath."

The twinkle in his eye, is quite plain for
both to see.

13.Cleansing the Soul

**Japanese baths,
Clean not the body,
But the soul.**

It is evening, both have passed their days separately and now Faron, is already soaking in the hot water of the deep, wooden, Hinoki cypress tub.

The simple wooden room, houses only the tub, with a large window facing it, a small stool, and a large bucket.

Jay enters, looking rather uncomfortable, he is wearing a yukata, a lightweight printed cotton kimono.

"Are we to get into the bath together, naked?"

"Only after you have washed properly."

"But the bath is for washing."

"Not here, in Japan. Washing is done outside, that is what the stool and bucket are for.

When you are clean, then you can join me, here in the bath, is where we relax."

The servant comes in and offers Jay a small towel.

"Isn't this a bit small for a towel?"

Fukuchō, laughs, a light, tinkle of a laugh. It is the first time that Benji, or Faron, for that matter, has heard her laugh.

"Silly, that is to cover your shame. It seems western men have something called modesty."

He doesn't have time to react as his kimono is unceremoniously slipped of his body, as the young girl starts to soap him all over.

After a moment of surprise, Jay realises
that he is quite enjoying the experience.

She then fills the bucket from the bath
and rinses the soap off. She does this
several times, leaving him a moment to
wash his private parts, before dousing
him several more times to confirm that all
the soap is off.

"Come, cousin, come and join me."

He keeps his modesty cloth carefully in
place.

"You must remove it before you get into
the water, it is not clean, so it must not
touch. Don't worry, I won't peek." 'Not
that I haven't seen you jack naked
before,' reflects Faron.

"Ahhh, that's good, but isn't it a bit hot?"

"It opens your pores and relaxes the
mind."

"So, now are you going to tell me what happened this morning? You could have gotten yourself killed."

"It was better than letting him kill you."

"But he might have killed you."

"I trusted that he wouldn't, and anyway, I wanted to fight him."

"You wanted to fight him? That big bully?"

"We used to be best friends."

"And then?"

"And then we kissed, once."

"And then what happened?"

"Then I wasn't welcome in their house anymore, and he stopped talking to me, not at all."

"But why?"

"I don't really know, but I think that it something to do with my being an orphan. At least that was what I think that he was saying, today."

"But you're not an orphan, you're my cousin. Your mother is my aunt."

"But you must never, never even mention that to anyone."

"You've lost me here. Why must I not tell anyone, that you are my cousin?"

"Because it would destroy my mother's reputation. And if she would lose her good name, she would not be able to earn any more money, and she would die, starving, homeless and destitute."

"So no one knows that you are her daughter?"

"She has no daughter."

"And you are okay with that?"

"She has always been there when I needed her. She got me into Rikihei's okiya, and she has also been my Okā-san, a type of mother for me.

And then she got someone to become my danna. A danna is a benefactor who makes the contract to pay for my training as a geisha girl."

"I'm not following."

"To become a geisha, is a very expensive thing. To begin with, we work in the house as servants, shikomi, but then we become minarai and then maiko.

We go to special schools, we learn things, eventually we no longer work in the house. We need kimono and make up, and other things that cost money, someone has to pay for all this."

"And the contract?"

"He, or she that owns our contract, owns us. They can decide what we do and who we do it with."

"Like a prostitute and her pimp."

"This word pimp, I do not understand, but a geisha does not sleep with her clients, she is not a prostitute. However, her virginity can often be auctioned off."

"How barbaric."

"Not at all, the Mizuage is a ceremony undergone by a maiko to signify her coming of age.

When the older geisha, that we call our Onei-san, our older sister, considers us ready to come of age, the topknot of our hair is symbolically cut. It is then that her virginity is auctioned off.

"Yeh, for some, fat old bastard to pocket a tidy sum."

"No, no. not at all, most of the money is for her, so that she can start off her life as a geisha, and maybe pay back a big part of her contract."

"Missooaige?"

"Mizuage, it means, hoisting from water."

"And, and you, you've done that?"

"There is no interest for bidding for the virginity of an orphan, someone of no family."

"It doesn't seem very fair."

"My day will come, 'ishi no ue nimo san nen', three years on the rock, be patient. Also, ryooyaku kuchi ni nigashi, Bitter pills may have welcome effects."

"And I also have some very important news."

"Yes, what important news?"

"I heard what he was talking about this
morning."

"Yes?"

"And I have been to the big chief guy this
afternoon and asked if I can marry
someone, I think that that is how it done
over here."

Before Fukuchō has a moment to react,
the servant of Aimatsu is ushered in.

"Aimatsu, has called for you, on a matter
of great importance. You must come
immediately."

"Excuse me," Fukuchō, slips a small
towel from somewhere, over certain parts
of her body as she jumps out of the bath,
and into her yukata.

"Good evening," she bows quickly to Jay,
"Benji-san."

14.Skeletons Emerge at Noon.

Hidden secrets
Rotting in cupboards
Stink.

"Please, come sit here, down beside me."

It had not taken long for Fukuchō to
dress, she had stopped bothering to paint
her face before going out, she had already
disgraced herself to the point where her
whole career as a geisha was already
likely to be finished.

And from there, she had hurried as fast as
she could to her mother's house.

Faron is surprised to find Maman, quietly
sitting on her tatami mat, with a tray of
tea, and two bowls, waiting besides her.

She seems most calm and composed.

It is mainly Faron who know his mother enough to know that this intense peacefulness, is more than likely hiding an enormous tempest of negativity.

People build the biggest, strongest dams, to hold back the most powerful pressures.

"Mother?"

"Benjamin has been to see the Daimyo this afternoon."

"Yes, I know."

"To ask to marry someone."

"That he has also told me."

"And did he, by chance, think to inform you, exactly to whom, he plans to marry?"

"We never got that far, your servant arrived just before he could tell me."

"So that leaves me the pleasure of sharing the news with you."

"So? So who does he wish to marry?"

"He has asked permission to marry … you!"

"Me? He can't think to do that. Can one marry one's cousin?"

"It is not unheard of."

"And you are okay that I marry my cousin?"

"You cannot marry Benjamin Pinkerton."

"Because?"

"Because, Benjamin Dole Pinkerton is your brother."

"My brother? It's not possible."

"To be precise, he is your half-brother."

“How is that possible?”

“Lieutenant Benjamin Franklin Pinkerton, was your father.”

“Oh. How do you know that Benji-san, has asked this?

“Father Fróis, Benjamin found him and asked his advice, and then asked him to organise the meeting and to accompany him to the castle.”

“And the Daimyo?”

“He has agreed, he seemed happy with the arrangement, as far as Father Fróis can tell.”

“What should I do, mother?”

“I don’t know. I am truly sorry for the pain and suffering that I have caused you. Maybe this is my punishment for not accepting the responsibility for what I have done.”

"What are you saying?"

"I am saying that I should have committed seppuku long ago."

"So, why didn't you?" Faron is surprised by the matter of fact fashion that she asks the question.

"For you. You had already lost a parent, and I reasoned to myself, even if it had to remain a secret amongst us, it was better for you that way, than with no parents, at all."

"So you have lived my whole life with this dishonour, to protect me?"

"What else is a mother to do?"

"I am truly honoured and blessed to have you as my mother."

"And I am blessed to have you as my daughter."

15. White, Pure Danger

Pure intent
Cuts through shame
Surely.

The garden is as it was, only days ago when Faron first appeared here.

The pretty, ornamental bridge over the ornamental crystal clear stream.

The beautiful trees, the faint hint of cherry blossom.

He is walking and talking to the monk.

"I don't know what will happen if you do this. Please reconsider, it seems to be a bad idea."

"There is no other way. It is decided."

"But have you thought about the consequences?"

"I have no idea what the consequences might be, 'cus you don't either."

"But, what about the pain?"

"Pain of dishonour is more unbearable."

"That is not Faron talking."

"I am also Fukuchō, this is my reality."

"And I can neither say nor do anything to dissuade you?"

"Goodbye, and thank you for all your help and support." And so Faron turns his back on the guide, and walks gently back towards the veranda.

She is calm, quiet, contented.
Her crisp, white kimono
Cracks, as she kneels
Underneath there is
A narrow obi sash.

She ties her knees
Tightly together,
That way, she
Cannot fall
Over.

She takes a small
Bowl of sake
Wine.

Raises up the bowl
Then, carefully
To her parted
Lips, and
Sips.

She then takes out a
Folded parchment
From inside her
Kimono.

Opens, and
Reads.

'My life has been
Closed by very
many heavy
Secrets
So
Now
I open
My life
My veins.'

She refolds the crisp
Parchment paper
Then places it
By her side.

The tantō
Is wrapped in
The whitest cloth.
The knife is
Sharp.

Jigaki will be
The noble
End.
Quickly
Severing the
Left, neck artery.

She opens
Her clothing
Revealing her
Vulnerable
Neck.

One slice
And …

"Noooo, Fukuchō, you must not!"

16.Skeletons Dance in the Sun

Frozen threats
Of Secrets, Melt
In the Sun.

"You have no right to stop me, mother."

"But **I** do!"

"Daimyo!" Her education can only allow her to bow, and to wait for his command to move.

"Up! Your mother might not have the right to impede your gesture of jigaki, but I do."

"Sire, I am the granddaughter of a samurai, I have the right to take my own life."

"You only have the rights that I choose to allow you. You see, I own your contract, I am your patron, I am your danna."

"Why are you her danna?"

"I do not have to answer to you."

"You are no longer my danna, I am an independent geisha, I can ask why you have her contract."

"Why I have the contract of your **daughter**?" The emphasis is clear to her.

She stops and looks round, Father Fróis has just appeared with Jay on tow. Not far behind them, Duncan and Mike rush in, their katana drawn and ready.

They take one look at the situation, drop their swords towards the floor and bow to their master.

"How do you know that?" She glares at the Father.

"I have many eyes and ears in this province, the good Father, is only just one of them. Now, child, please explain the reason for this noble act."

"I, I'm sorry but I cannot."

"It's okay, daughter, it is about time that I stopped hiding my shame and my love.

Fukuchō cannot marry Benjamin because they have the same father, they are half-brother and sister.

"Then I was too late?"

"Too late for what?" But before the lord could answer to the mother, the half-brother bursts out.

"What are you talking about? I couldn't marry her, even if she was just my cousin, I couldn't marry my own cousin."

"Then why did you ask the Daimyo to marry me?"

"But I didn't I said, 'Wochi wa kekk and shit aides you, Fuku chiyo. Which, I hope means that, 'I want to marry Fukuchiyo."

"But that's my name, sort of, Fukuchō".

"No it isn't, it's mine, Fukichiyo." Of course, it would have to be Tessa.

"But why would you be marrying Benji-san?" Faron would also like to know this.

"Because he bought out my contract, so he is danna. I went to thank him for his generous act, I just fell in love with him.

We cannot speak much yet, but Father Fróis has offered to help us both to learn each other's language."

"Benji-san, why did you buy Fukichiyo's contract?" Fukuchō is also more than intrigued.

"But I have no idea of what anyone's talking about, I haven't bought anything, I don't think so."

"Hmm, hmm."

"Father Fróis?"

"Your excellence?"

"You wish to say something?"

"Not really. Although, more than anyone, I should know that confession is good for the soul.

Benjamin didn't buy out Fukichiyo's contract, that money came from his father, Lieutenant Pinkerton."

"Why would he wish to buy out my contract?"

"He didn't, he wished to buy out his daughter's contract.

His lawyer wrote me a letter, which arrived on the same boat as his son, the post arrived with the dingy that announced its arrival.

He had asked the lawyer, if anything were to happen to him to hunt out the owner of her contract and buy it out for her as a last gesture of her absent father.

He had often planned to return and to do it himself, but the moment never arrived.

But when I found out that the contract was held by Shimazu Yoshihisa and knowing how jealous he already was of your relationship with Pinkerton, frankly, I feared for your life and of Fukuchō.

So I wetted the paper and smudged the name so that it might be read as Fukichiyo's, if the Daimyo should suspect that Pinkerton was **her** father, then it wouldn't have carried the same risk. ”

"Why would my danna, ever want to hurt
me?" The great man takes out his fan,
and strolls off towards the scented trees.

"Shimazu Yoshihisa, why might my
daughter be in danger if you knew that
she was the daughter of Lieutenant
Pinkerton?"

"Father Fróis, you seem to be good at
explaining things, please tell them."

"Everything?"

"I will be inside, drinking tea." And he
enters into the house. All eyes fall onto
the religious man.

"Shimazu Yoshihisa has always been in
love with you," he nods towards Maman.

"When you started your relationship with
Pinkerton, he hoped that it was just a
business arrangement between you.

But when it became clear that it was getting serious, he summoned me to go and suggest to your sister, that she should be the one to be married to him.

He promised her, that if she would make such a request, he would support it.

From then on, I have carried the guilt of this ignoble act. Of course it became even worse when you confessed to me that you had had a child. So I did what I could, in an effort to repair for my sins.

After Benjamin was born, I took it upon myself to convince you, Aimatsu to let me share with Butterfly that you had a daughter, but that I was not aware of who the father was.

Which has been true until today, although, I must admit to have always having had my suspicions.

I then convinced them both to let the children play together.

At least the children would have a contact, and I had hoped that sooner or later, the sisters could make peace.

I am not sure how Shimazu Yoshihisa found out that Fukuchō was your daughter, I honestly believe that it didn't come me.

But as soon as he knew, he informed Madame Rikihei-san, that he would finance her training as a geisha, that he would create a contract and become her danna.

I then asked his permission to intervene, in his name, with Miyamoto Hanzō, being a close neighbour, to allow Fukuchō to be welcomed into their house and to play with Hattori.

Again, my desire to help and repair something created more problems."

"What problems are you speaking of, Father?"

"The relationship between your daughter and Hattori."

"There is no relationship between us. I was thrown out of their house. I hate him."

"Which is even worse for my conscience, for you see, Hattori is in love with you."

Before she can even begin to respond, the other person in question bursts in.

"I'm not in love with her. Who could I love a wild orphan like that?"

"No, Hattori, remember, she is not an orphan, and I had no right to stop your love for her.

Fukuchō, please, I must apologise, it was my choice to ban you from our house. I could not, for honour, allow my son to marry someone of whom we knew neither the identity, neither of the father, nor even of the mother."

"Love when impossible to manifest can turn to hatred. Again that was a further sin that I was forced to assume."

"Father, you seem to have tried to have done your best."

"Thank you, for that, my child, but it doesn't end there."

"No, it doesn't, but it wasn't all your fault. For you see, Pinkerton leaving Japan was my fault."

Jay, succeeding to follow the conversations thanks to the combined efforts of the two Faron's, suddenly jumps in. "Why, why did my father choose to leave Japan?"

Maman, who does understand English quite well, responds immediately, and in English.

"Because I informed him, quite soon after your sister was born, about her and that he was the father.

He wanted to acknowledge her but he was already married to Butterfly, so it was impossible. There would have been an enormous scandal, and no one would have come out of it well.

So I insisted that he never saw you. He said that he couldn't stand to watch you growing up, but not be able to talk to you, so he took a commission to return back to his own country."

"So it was my fault that he abandoned Benji?"

"He didn't know that Butterfly was pregnant, he asked me, as his Father confessor, to ask Shimazu Yoshihisa as Daimyo to dissolve the marriage, but I didn't have courage to do that, straight away.

And before I was brave enough to think to do the deed, Butterfly announced that she was pregnant, and after that, well it was just impossible.

But you cannot trouble yourself with any guilt, just because you were born."

"Then how did he find out about me?"

"Once again it fell to me to link the stories. Your father kept a correspondence with me, so he could have news of his daughter, and from time to time would send some money.

The money I would often give to Okā-san Rikihei, who would then use it to buy Fukuchō a new kimono or some such frippery, but sometimes I would buy you a present with it.

I would tell Butterfly that it was money from the church, and that she had to accept it as such.

Things worked reasonably well for a few years, but your mother was becoming more and more desperate that Pinkerton was not coming back. So, once again, I chose to intervene, I wrote to him and told him that he had a son that he had never met.

He wrote back that he couldn't come straight away, but he would not rest until he had returned and claimed his son.

And so, it was again through my clumsy efforts that he came back to Japan."

"But he only came for me, he didn't came back for her. He never, ever loved her, he was just manipulated into marrying her."

"That isn't totally true. Yes, he was manipulated into marrying her, and to begin with her pleasure was having stolen him from me, and he seemed to have found us quite interchangeable.

But when he returned, things became
more complicated, for you see, he came
to see me, the day that she died.

Because of what happened afterwards,
that conversation, has become one that I
have replayed, over and over in my mind.
I can repeat it word for word."

The others, having no means to
understand, other than crowding around
Father Fróis, and not feeling that this
story was their business, discretely
retired.

However, not before the courteous father
and son had brought two stools for the
two women to sit down on.

17.Before the Sun Set

**A stolen heart
Is broken, or
Returned.**

"It was already quite late in the afternoon,
he had spent most of the morning
preparing for his passage home. It was
the first time that he had returned to my
house since I had informed him about
your birth.

He came to inform me that he had come
back to take Dole, as he called him, back
with him. That I was already aware of,
and ready for, what I was not prepared for
was what followed …

'I suppose that you know that I have
come to take Dole, back home.'

'So I have been informed.'

'I am also going to take my daughter
back, too.'

169

'What are you saying? You cannot think
to take Fukuchō, she's my daughter.'

'She is being brought up as an orphan. I
won't have my daughter living of the
charity of a woman that trains
prostitutes.'

'How dare you say such a thing? Okā-san
Rikihei, was my okā-san, so you take me
for a prostitute?'

'Listen, my beautiful pine tree, (my name
means, girl whose love is as steadfast as
the pines), I didn't mean that at all.'

'But you think that Fukuchō is being
trained to be a prostitute?'

'I've never really understood what being
a geisha means.'

'A geisha is an artist, not a prostitute.'

'Okay, okay, so she's not being trained to
be a prostitute.

But she is still being brought up as an orphan. She doesn't know who her parents are.'

'There you are wrong, she does know who her mother is, she knows who her aunty is, and she knows who her cousin is. But she also knows that she must never, ever tell anyone of that.'

'Oh, anyway, she needs a proper education, and she needs to know who her father is.'

'She is having a decent education, but she certainly doesn't need to know a father that she has never met, and has only returned because he has found out that he has a son. You are not taking my daughter, and if you try, I will kill you where you stand.'

'I suppose that you would too, wouldn't you?'

'Do you want to see how the daughter of a samurai defends her family?'

'Fine, you can keep her, but I call it selfishness. She would do better to have a decent western education, like her brother.'

'But you could leave him here, Butterfly needs her son, please, please don't take him.'

'That is not your business, I have already discussed it with Butterfly, it is already decided, Dole's clothes are already packed. So, if that's everything, I have to go.'

'Wait, just one more thing.'

'Yes?'

'Before you go, please tell me, did you ever love me? Even a little?'

'Yes, yes I loved you, and, and more than just a little.'

'But you accepted to marry Butterfly.'

'Just like you, I couldn't go against Shimazu Yoshihisa, I had no choice. Either I married her, or he would have had me thrown out of Japan. I would lose you anyway.'

'But you were willing to marry Butterfly to stay in the country.'

'I was sent here to open up diplomatic and commercial links with Japan. If I got thrown out, then I would have failed my mission and my country would have lost an important opportunity. '

'Then you are a monster, you never really loved me, nor, even did you love Butterfly.'

'My love for you I succeeded to transfer to her. You are alike enough for me to forget that it was her, and to imagine that it was you.

After a while, I ceased to make the difference, and just loved her and you, as much the same person.'

'So you did love Butterfly?'

'…. I still do.'

'More than your wife from the West?'

'That was also an arranged marriage, of sorts.'

'But do you love her?'

'… I still do.'

'Still do?'

'Yes, yes, I do still love her. Fool, fool, fool that I am.

Always trying to prove that I can be
successful, and throwing away the only
things of any value.

Yes, yes, Aimatsu, I do still love you, but
more than that, I am in love with
Butterfly.'

And then he rushed out,
    but of course,
        he was too late.

18. Turning of the Collar

The air vibrates with the music of the small hummingbird hawk-moths, gaily sucking on the simple white honeysuckle, climbing the length of the house.

The gentle fragrance of the cherry blossom, still floats in the breeze.

Fukuchō is dressed in a simple, black kimono; wearing the white shironuri makeup and traditional geisha hair style.

She carries in one hand an object called a kagura suzu, divine entertainment bells; made of three tiers of bells, three on the top, five in the middle, and seven on the bottom.

The garden has a number of stools set round, facing the veranda.

It is not usual to have so many people present for the erikae, the graduation ceremony of a geisha.

This first part is traditionally only for members of her okiya, but as there are only Madame Rikihei, Fukichiyo and Maru from her house, it has been decided that other close friends be invited.

And, as one of the most important guests is Shimazu Yoshihisa the Daimyo himself, no-one would dare to question this move from strict tradition.

Fukichiyo, is Fukuchō's, onei-san or older sister, it was with her that she has learned the craft of being a geisha, and it will be with her that she will pass from maiko to geisha.

Maru brings out a tray. On which are stacked three orange-reddish lacquered bowls and a pot of sake. The three bowls are all of different sizes, the smallest, logically being on the top.

Fukichiyo takes the top bowl, and fills it with some sake.

"Heaven," she takes a sip and passes it to Fukuchō's, who also takes a sip before passing it back to her older sister, who takes a second sip. She then passes it back to Fukuchō's, and then again until they have each drunk three times from the bowl.

She then takes the second bowl.

"Earth," and again they both drink three times from the second bowl.

"Humankind," and for the third time, they both drink three times from the third bowl.

And so the ritual, San-san-ku-do, or three-three-nine-times, has been correctly performed.

"I now will honour you with your new geisha name, from now you will be known as … Matsuko, child of the pine tree."

Fukuchō cannot resist a quick glance towards her mother, Aimatsu is energetically fanning herself, but she cannot hide the tears of joy, of finally being openly and officially recognised as her daughter's mother.

It is now time for Fukuchō to perform a dance for the attendees.

Faron has a passing moment of doubt, but as dancing is something that Fukuchō has been trained in since early childhood, he feels her confidence, and relaxes, ready to experience being a poised and practised dancer.

Maru begins to play the flute and Fukuchō, using the kagura suzu bells as an accompaniment, re-enacts the part of a Shinto story.

It is in the story where Amaterasu, the
goddess of the sun, is tricked into coming
out of the heavenly rock cave, where she
had chosen to hide.

To return to the heavens, and let the
divine light, reign down, once again.

And hence, the traditional part of the
erikae, or turning of the collar, from red
to white, has been accomplished.

Now everyone is served sake, and
Fukuchō is finally, a fully, fledged
geisha.

19.More turning.

Plant a tree
Feed it your love
Eat the fruit.

The final bow and Faron allows himself
to feel the joy and relief of the end of the
ceremony.

They will still be officially responsible
for the rest of the celebration, but in
reality, as the guest of honour, Fukuchō,
now known as Matsuko, will have little to
do.

"Come, my beautiful daughter, please
come and sit next to me," Aimatsu, being,
in both realities the mother, comes to take
her child, openly, to come and sit next to
her.

"Mother, are you feeling well?" The fan
is out, sweeping across her face, as if to
swat the invisible bugs, which are getting
into her eyes.

"I am so happy and proud to be your mother."

This seems to Faron, to be the first time, ever, that he had heard his mother say these words, and, miracle of miracles, while expressing the appropriate emotion.

He is struck, as if by an enormous ball of soft, sweet, pink, candy floss. His body becomes sticky and gooey; his breathing is blocked by the sugary air, which he is trying to inhale.

He is aware that his female other, is also experiencing waves of joy, but his pleasure, largely supersedes, hers.

To feel the bright, warm sun's rays, after a whole lifetime of living under clouds and rain, is to be transported over the rainbow, but with no wicked witches in sight.

Neither can walk safety, unaided, but slightly leaning on each other, they manage to return to their places.

However, on returning, Aimatsu finds her seat has been moved, as has that of her ward.

"It seems that it is once again my duty to intervene in your lives."

"Father?"

"Your stool has been placed besides that of Shimazu Yoshihisa, and that of Matsuko, next to Hattori Hanzō."

"Why?" Both women ask, in unison.

"That was the order of your Daimyo." He bows to them both, turns and goes to talk to Jay.

She approaches her lord, "kimi?" Bows and waits.

"Please, come and sit by me. I believe
that there subjects that we must discuss,"

They begin to talk; first, he informs that
he has taken over the expenses of this
okiya, out of appreciation for the way that
Matsuko has been looked after.

He then passes over to her, her daughter's
contract, she would know best how to
handle this difficult, headstrong, young
women.

Then he leans further towards her, their
voices soft and secretive.

They both take out their fans, and protect
their faces, with sure, swift, flicks of the
wrist.

The stroboscopic effect of the fans,
partially masks their countenances,
helping to protect something of the
emotions, that they are having difficulty
from expressing.

She passes the yellow fan
From her right hand,
To her left.
Then,
Relieved
Of its burden,
Discreetly lets it
Drop.
Down,
Down to
That side
Of her body.
Accidentally ,
Brushing the hand,
Against that other hand,
That, of the older man.
Worlds transform,
Through such
Accidents.

Matsuko, arrives at the stool, set aside for
her. Hattori, is talking to his father, he is
feigning to have not seen her.

Faron does not take lightly to this obvious
rudeness, but he has no power to control
this body, so he has no other option but to
stand, patiently, and wait.

Hattori nods to Miyamoto, who bids his
son farewell, gets up and leaves. He then
turns towards Matsuko, who, against
every impulse in Faron's being, bows
deeply to Hattori, and waits.

"You may sit."

"Thank you Hattori-san." A silence
follows. It is not for her to speak now, she
must wait, respectfully for the man to
continue.

"You have dishonoured me, and yourself
by appearing without your white
shironuri makeup and fighting with me,
passing yourself off as a samurai male."

"I apologise most humbly, Hattori-san,"

Faron is seething with anger, but yet, he can feel that she is calm inside. No, not just calm, confident, in control.

'This is a game, you are playing a game with him. You are not really apologising, you are in no way sorry for what you have done. You know that he needs to keep his honour, he has to keep face.

So, he must criticise you, and you have to apologise to him, but you know, you know that he is in love with you.

And because he loves you, now you can control him, but your love for him means that he must always believe that he is the master and you are the servant.

He is the dog, and you are the tail. But this tail, wags the dog. Now I think I finally, really understand the song lyrics, 'a boy chases a girl, until she catches him'.

“Good, it is important that you are aware of the wrong that you have done us both.”

“I have been lacking the firm hand of a man in my life.”

‘And so the trap, opens.’

“That is clear enough to see.”

“I have never had a father to keep me on the right path.”

‘Keep going.’

“You need a man to direct you.”

“That is true.”

“Fortunately for you, it is now known that you, at least, come from honourable families.”

“I am fortunate about that.”

"Even if your conduct, of late, leaves much to be desired."

"I have truly not behaved as I should have."

"It would still be a great sacrifice for a man of good family to accept you into their family."

"It would take a man of courage and honour."

"I have taken the step to have discussed this with my father, who is a man of the highest standing."

"Yes, Hattori-san."

'Still working on the one-down position.'

"And he agrees with me, that it would be a most charitable act, to offer to take you into our family."

"And a great honour, for me."

'Don't push it too far, minx.'

"So it is agreed?"

"Thank you to you, and to your father."

He is just about to go, when Father Fróis, standing on the veranda, gives another of his theatrical type coughs.

"Hmm, hmm. If I could have your attention, for just a moment or two, I would like to say a few words."

Everyone stops and turns to the priest.

"This has been a very eventful few days, and I would like to take a moment to reflect on the sense of what has happened.

Many of us have been holding secrets, secrets that have been hiding away, for many years.

Secrets that have done us much harm, secrets that have also, directly or indirectly harmed others. I would like to talk about sin.

Holding a secret, is not in itself a sin, far from it. Many secrets are held to protect ourselves or to protect others. But when holding that secret goes against part of our moral code, that is where it becomes a sin.

The Hebrew word most often translated as "sin" in our English Bibles is the word chata'ah, which means "missing the mark," as an archer might miss his target when shooting an arrow.

When we act in such a way, as we miss our own moral targets, then this is a sin. It is a sin because who we choose to be and how we would choose to act, are distant from how we have been or acted.

It is that separation from our God self,
and our reality that causes pain,
emotional and spiritual.

Peace comes when you admit your sins,
when you acknowledge that separation.

Yesterday, I have spoken my truth, and I
have set myself free from the suffering of
many years, as have many of you.

How come has it been that I have been
allowed, no, admittedly forced, to tell this
truth?

The reason for this, is you, you Matsuko,
Fukuchō. Your willingness to sacrifice
yourself, even unto death, to protect those
that you love, has been the key to my
salvation.

And so I thank you, for all of us. Today,
you have officially become a woman, but
you have, in reality, been more than a
mother to us, to us all.

I salute you, Matsuko-san, thank you."
And he bows deeply, in her direction.

She slowly gets to her feet, and then, with
the utmost care and respect, returns the
bow to the good Father.

Then she turns to her danna, but even
before she can repeat the action,
something extraordinary happens.

The fan cuts across the air, 'stop', 'don't
move'. This imperial gesture is well
known to all. To move now, even the
slightest shift of weight from one leg to
other, could mean death.

Nobody moves.
The silence is total.
Maybe, nobody is even breathing.
What has happened?
What could have upset the Daimyo?
Who was have angry with?
Would this happy moment
End, even in tragedy?

All eyes, rest on the great and terrible man.

Slowly, carefully, he replaces his fan in his obi sash.

He takes several, measured, deep breathes.

He then elegantly raises himself, from his stool.

And turns to face Faron, full on.

And bows.

Fukuchō is petrified, she is so shocked and surprised, she is incapable to move.

Fortunately, Hattori has lost neither his presence of mind, nor his sense of propriety.

He digs her painfully in the side of her ribs.

The shock of his gesture immediately awakens her from her stupor, and she deeply bows in acknowledgement.

J. J. straightens up, inclines his head, slightly, and regains his seat.

Faron's head is spinning.

That was his father.

His father that was never satisfied with anything that he had ever done in his life.

His father, rich and powerful, head of a small empire.

His father, in this world, lord of all he surveyed.

His father that had just bowed to him, and in public.

His father had finally, publicly, acknowledged him.

He had graduated with first class honours,

He had won the cup, the shield, the first
prize,

He had the Emmy, Golden Globe, the
Oscar

The bronze, silver and gold.

Pride and pleasure burst from his heart,
exploding like the greatest fireworks
display of all time.

Almost mechanically, she continued to
appreciate and to bow to; their mother,
Hattori, Madame Rikihei, Fukichiyo and
then Maru.

Finally, she walks up to Benjamin.

"I understand, that you do something that
called a 'hug', in families in the west,
how is it done?"

Of course, Faron knows full well, but it is Fukuchō, (as he still thinks of her), that is asking the question.

Jay walks up to Faron, and gently, but firmly takes him in his arms, and hugs him.

Tears well up, and dribble down; creating rivulets of hot, grey streams, flowing down the snowy white expanse of her painted face.

Faron sobs, never has he ever expected to be hugging, or hugged by Jay, not ever, ever again.

An ocean of pleasure, wells up from deep, deep down, inside him.

'Please, please, please, don't, ever, ever stop.' But of course it does, and the moment passes.

20.Final Curtain

An object
That is priceless, is
Not worthless.

"So, have you been able to reconnect to pleasure?"

"Yes, thank you. I think that I had to believe that I deserved it."

"You certainly were ready to sacrifice yourself for others."

"It just seemed to be the only thing to do, but now that I have time to think back, I realise that I still don't deserve all that appreciation and stuff."

"I'm not following you. You were ready to sacrifice your life to protect others."

"No, not really. First of all, if I were to die, here, in this world, where I don't even truly exist.

What would be the worst that could happen? I would just start this level again, like a really complicated, video game.

I have succeeded the first island, so that's done, it's in the pocket. So I would just start this island again, even going back to Venice, wouldn't so be bad, to do over."

"And the pain of committing seppuku?"

"But it wasn't seppuku, it was to be jigaki. Jigaki is slicing the arteries of the neck, just one, quick stroke it seems a swift and certain death, totally unlike the slow and painful death of seppuku, slicing the stomach, and all."

"But you couldn't be sure. And yet you chose to take the risk, anyway. And then there was the sword challenge, you could have gotten very badly hurt. In both instances, you risked great suffering to protect someone else."

“No I didn’t.”

“What are you saying? Of course you did.”

“No, you don’t understand. It was her, she was controlling what I was doing. Yes, I agreed for the stuff, but it wasn’t my motivation, it wasn’t my wish or desire. Underneath, I’m still a selfish coward.

Yes, I have found back the ability to experience pleasure, and for that, I thank you.

I never thought that I could feel that good about anything, not ever again. In that, at least, this has to be considered as a success.”

“So we agree that you have felt pleasure?”

“No questions there.”

"But that you still feel that you don't deserve all this acknowledgement?"

"I know that I don't deserve it."

"You don't seem to have much esteem, for yourself."

"Why should I have? I've never really done anything to deserve it."

"And if you had done things to deserve being appreciated?"

"Then that would be great, wouldn't it?"

"Could you just do something for me?"

"Sure."

"Just close your eyes, for a moment."

Faron closes his eyes.

The effect is quite strange.

The stool, on which he is sitting seems to have become unstable.

It seems to be rocking slightly, forwards and backwards.

Suddenly, there is a brilliant light shining down on him.

He almost loses his balance.

"Careful!" The guide screams into his ear. "Or you're going to fall off of your horse."

Gentle reader, thank you for purchasing this book and I very much hope that you have enjoyed it.

If so, please help others to make the choice to read this by sharing your views with your friends and writing a review on Amazon.

Thank you,

Kindest regards

Gary

Other works

By

Gary Edward Gedall

Island of Serenity Book 1
The Island of Survival

Pierre-Alain James 'Faron' Ferguson is about to commit suicide, in his suicide note he attempts to understand how he has come to have wrecked not only his own life, but also all of those around him.

Pierre-Alain James 'Faron' Ferguson finds himself in a type of 'no-mans-land', between here and there, he must accept to visit the 7 islands before he will be allowed to continue on to his next steps. The islands are named; Survival, Pleasure, Esteem, Love, Expression, Insight and lastly, the Island of Serenity

The Early Years:
Pierre-Alain James 'Faron' Ferguson is born into a well-to-do household of a factory owner, Scottish father and mother of a noble French family

He, and his younger brother Jay, grow up in a home of two distant but invested parents. Already, the first, small stones of his future problems are being put into place.

The Island of Survival:
Faron finds himself on the first of the seven islands, transformed into a prehistoric human form, he must learn how to interact with the local environment and the early humanoid tribe.

Here, he must reconnect with his instinct of survival.

Island of Serenity Book 2
Sun & Rain

This is the second chapter of Faron's life history, in which he falls in love, becomes a real cowboy, starts boarding school, finds his two best friends, and more than that would be telling too much.

FREE: If you have not yet read Book 1, Survival, no worries, I have included a shortened version, so as to introduce you to the story and the main characters.

Island of Serenity Book 3
The Island of Pleasure
Vol 1

Part 1.

Faron finds himself in a past version of Venice, as the owner of an old but grand hotel that doubles as the meeting place for the wealthy men of the City and the high class escort girls that live in the establishment.

Faron can do anything that he likes without limitation or cost. Not only can he avail himself of the girls, but can eat and drink, without limit, but never suffer from a hangover, nor gain a gram.

So why has the enigmatic guide brought him here, and will his limitless access to life's offerings really bring him the pleasure that he is destined to experience?

Part 2.

 Faron is transformed into an adolescent tom boy. In this more modern version of Venice, 'he' has just 7 days to be made into a high class escort girl.

What does this experience and the intrigues of the other persons within his sphere, mean for him, on his continuing quest to understand, and to experience, Pleasure?

Island of Serenity Book 5
Rise and Fall

In this the 5th book of the series, we watch as Faron
grows from an adolescent into a young, driven man.

He begins by escaping to New York, before starting
his University career, finding back his two school,
best friends, Duncan and Mike.

After graduating, the three find themselves setting up
a business, manufacturing, buying and importing
goods from Indonesia.

Success seems to be just around the corner, but Faron
cannot help himself. Bitterness and betrayal, hound
him like a hungry dog.

To destroy, his own best friend, is not an act to take
lightly, but take it, he does.

And what of Angelique, and his daughter Aideen?
He is still emotionally entangled, but is that a good
thing, or a very bad thing?

Only time will tell.

Tasty Bites

(Series – published or in preproduction)

Face to Face	A young teacher asks to befriend an older colleague on Face Book, "I have a very delicate situation, for which I would appreciate your advice"
Free 2 Luv	The e-mail exchanges between; RichBitch, SecretLover, the mother, the bestie, and the lawyer, expose a complicated and surprising story
Love you to death	A toy town parable, populated by your favourite playthings, about the dangerous game of dependency and co-dependency
Master of all Masters	In an ancient land, the disciples argue about who is the Master of all Masters. The solution is to create a competition

Pandora's Box	If you had a magic box, into which you could bury all your negative thoughts and feelings, wouldn't that be wonderful?
Shame of a family	Being born different can be a heavy burden to bear. Especially for the family
The Noble Princess	If you were just a humble Saxon, would you be good enough to marry a noble Norman Princess?
The Ugly Barren Fruit Tree	A weird foreign tree that bears no fruit, in an apple orchard. What value can it possibly have?
The Woman of my Dreams	What would you do, if the woman that you fell in love with in your dream, suddenly appears in real life?

Adventures with the Master

Dhargey was a sickly child or so his parents treated him. He was too weak to join the army or work in the fields or even join the monastery as a normal trainee monk.

To explain to the 'Young Master' why he should be accepted into the order with a lightened program, he was forced to accompany the revered old man a little ways up the mountain.

As his parents watched him leave; somewhere they felt that they would never see their sickly, fragile boy ever again, somewhere they were totally right.

He was a happy, healthy seven year old until he witnessed the riders, dressed in red and black, destroying his village and murdering his parents; the trauma cut deep into his psyche.

Only the chance meeting with a wandering monk could set him back onto the road towards health and serenity.

Through meditation, initiations, stories, taming wild horses, becoming a monkey, mastering the staff and the sword; the future 'Young Master' prepares to face his greatest demon.

Two men, two journeys, one goal.

The Tales of Peter the Pixie

Peter the innocent, honest, young pixie, and his friends;
Elli, the, 'much older then she looks', modest but powerful
Fairy, Timothy, the old, trustworthy, Toad and the, ever so
noble, Fire Dragon, are the best of friends.

Together, they experience many wonderful and heart-
warming adventures.

Told in a classical children's story style; Peter and his
friends, meet all kinds of creatures and situations.

As with all children, Peter is often confronted with
experiences that he does not know how best to deal with,
and he often reacts in ways that are not the most
appropriate. Fortunately; with the help of his good friends,
good will and common sense, everything always turns out
for the best.

None Fiction:

The Zen Approach to Modern Living Vol 1

Fundamentals, Family & Friends

Life is often experienced as a series of conflicts and aggressions, both from the outside and within ourselves.

The Zen Approach to Modern Living series, will lead you towards a more harmonious way of dealing with the many, complex and competing elements of your daily life.

These conflicts leave us exhausted, depressed, angry, and feeling generally unhappy and unfulfilled.

Being more in harmony with yourself will bring more happiness, more energy and open up the route to self-fulfillment.

Volume 1 covers; an introduction to the basic concepts, our relationship with ourselves, our family, (partner, children, parents, brothers, sisters and in-laws), friends and enemies.

Plus, plus, plus, A Bonus Chapter: My Deepest, Darkest, Secret.

The Zen approach to Low Impact Training and Sports

A simple method for achieving a healthy body and a healthy mind

Many of us approach our fitness and sports activities in an aggressive and competitive fashion.

And even if we feel that we succeed to break out of our comfort zones and win against ourselves or our opponent, there is an important cost to bear.

This level of violence that we have come to accept, so as to reach our goals is also an aggression against ourselves. By removing this need to 'win at any price', and tuning in with our bodies and emotions, we can achieve an enormous amount, all the while being in harmony with our mind, body and spirit.

The Zen approach to Low Impact Training and Sports, is a new softer approach where you can have the best of all worlds.

REMEMBER

Stories and poems for self-help and self-development
based on techniques of Ericksonian and auto-hypnosis

Dusk falls, the world shrinks little by little into a smaller and smaller circle as the light continues to diminish.
The centre of this world is illuminated by a small, crackling sun; the flames dance, and the rough faces of the people gathered there are lit by the fire of their expectations.
The old man will begin to speak, he will explain to them how the world is, how it was, how it was created. He will help them understand how things have a sense, an order, a way that they need to be.
He will clarify the sources of un-wellness and unhappiness, what is sickness, where it comes from, how to notice it and... how to heal it.
To heal the sick, he will call forth the forces of the invisible realms, maybe he will sing, certainly he will talk, and talk, and talk.

Since the beginning of time we have gathered round those
who can bring us the answers to our questions and the means
to alleviate our sufferings.
This practice has not fundamentally changed since the earliest times; in every era, continent and culture we have found and continue to find these experiences.

In this, amongst the oldest of the healing traditions, he has succeeded to meld modern therapy theories and techniques with stories and poems of the highest quality.

With much humanity, clinical vignettes, common sense and lots of humour, the reader is gently carried from situation to situation. Whether the problems described concern you directly, indirectly or not at all, you will surely find interest and benefits from the wealth of insights and advices contained within and the conscious or unconscious positive changes through reading the stories and poems.

Picturing the Mind

Vol 1

A simple model capable to explain the functioning and dysfunctioning of the human psyche.

Introduction to the Field theory of Human Functioning

For the average man and woman in the street, the complex and competing theories and models of the human psyche; its development, functioning and dis-functioning are often unhelpful for their understanding of themselves.

This becomes even more problematic when they find themselves in difficulty, as often, even the mental health professionals, who are experts in their own fields, find themselves at a loss to communicate successfully how and why the patent is unwell and what needs to happen to find or regain a healthy balance.

This opens up the question; 'is it possible to image a simple, single model, accessible to everyone, to explain the development, functioning and dis-functioning of the human psyche?'

One that builds on existing theories and models, benefitting from the mass of experience and research of 'modern western' psychological concepts and ideas, but also integrating traditional visions of the human psyche and modern theories from the physical sciences.

Picturing the Mind, is an attempt to answer to this need.

Picturing the Mind
Vol 2

The second volume following on from the initial concepts will reflect on such subjects as:
Relationships
Exchanging energy
Heart & Soul
Recuperation
Subjective constructions
An unconscious yes, an unconscious no
Me, myself and everyone else
Circles in circles, the micro level
Circles in circles, the macro level
Intuition
Metaphysical reflections

Picturing the Mind

Vol 3

Will deal with:

Psychopathology

Traditional psychotherapy
&
Alternative therapeutic approaches.